PIECES OF A DREAM

PIECES OF A DREAM

Sy Makaringe

Illustrations by Len Sak

PENGUIN BOOKS

PENGUIN BOOKS

Published by the Penguin Group
27 Wrights Lane, London W8 5TZ, England
Viking Penguin, a division of Penguin Books USA Inc, 375 Hudson Street,
New York, New York 10014, USA
Penguin Books Australia Ltd, Ringwood, Victoria, Australia
Penguin Books Canada Ltd, 10 Alcorn Avenue, Toronto, Ontario,
Canada M4V 3B2
Penguin Books (NZ) Ltd, 182–190 Wairau Road, Auckland 10, New Zealand
Penguin Books South Africa (Pty) Ltd, Pallinghurst Road, Parktown,
South Africa 2193

Penguin Books South Africa (Pty) Ltd, Registered Offices: 20 Woodlands
Drive, Woodmead, Sandton 2128

First published by Penguin Books 1996

Cover illustration by Len Sak
Reproduction, printed and bound by The Rustica Press (Pty) Ltd,
Old Mill Road, Ndabeni

D5028

This book is dedicated to my son
Sandile Mikateko 'Madala' Makaringe;
ngwenya ya ka hina, ngwenya ya ka Makaringe.

CONTENTS

PREFACE

There are millions of things that happen in ordinary people's lives, things that make up what is known as living and which are reported in the mass media. These things leap into your eyes from newspaper pages or jump from the television screen into your living rooms in the form of pictures, graphics, text and sound – from morning till evening. These things are called news. They can be assimilated or rejected. They can educate or mislead. The question is, how often does news entertain? Obviously this question may be treated as a statement and not a moot point for intellectual debate, as the operative phrase is to entertain.

Here is a quiz, though. Why is it that people will never remember without prodding whether, when the robot turns green, the green light is on top or at the bottom?

Briefly, given that the above is a successful redefinition of journalism, you might say *Pieces of a Dream* is precisely about that – it deals with those mundane things that often go unnoticed because they are deliberately obscured by the too rigid formalities of the journalist's grind. Facts, balance etc. It is indeed true, no matter how hard they may deny it, that many South Africans have had it up to here with the type of news they are fed daily. This point need not be laboured. To use a cliché – the people want to put a smile on the horizon.

This collection of pieces from Sy Makaringe's popular satirical column 'Whispers' in the *Sowetan* newspaper is a successful redefinition of journalism. It has succeeded in focusing on the lighter side of serious issues, especially during these times of transformation and transition. At the end of the day, one cannot help but smile at a grave situation.

Pieces of a Dream is not political but it is about politics. It is not sexist but it is about sexism. It is an observation, a picture that forms in the eye of this journalist but transcends the orthodox and conventional journalese. It forces the reader to wear the same hat but in a different way.

Common, rather than conventional reporting is blunt and to the point. It gives you information quickly as though you are about to disembark at the next station. It leaves you either more knowledgeable or poorer where information is concerned. But it is this convention which *Pieces of a Dream* expertly manipulates to make the reader sit back and ponder admiringly, even when the bus is about to offload its mass of bodies in a hurry to fetch another batch. *Pieces of a Dream* is destined to entertain. It does not pretend to chronicle the black people's hardships or the causes thereof. That kind of writing is already a lucrative industry.

Themba Molefe
Johannesburg
February 1996

ACKNOWLEDGEMENTS

This book would not have been possible had it not been for the collective support of the following: *Sowetan* Editor-in-Chief Aggrey Klaaste, *Sowetan* itself and New Africa Publications for giving me permission to use this collection of articles. Joe Thloloe, former Managing Editor of *Sowetan* who is now a *makhulu baas* at the SABC. He played the pivotal role of a midwife (or should that be midperson or midhusband?) as he was there during the embryonic and infancy stages of my column in the said newspaper. He always gave me a pat on the back whenever I did a good thing and a stern word of advice when I faltered. Len Sak, a cartoonist whose brilliant and imaginative illustrations give this book a lift and make it more exciting to read. Don Mattera, a veteran journalist, distinguished poet and political activist. His advice and fatherly encouragement will always mean a lot to me. Sam Muofhe, a friend and successful businessman. He has always been there for me every time I have needed his support. My colleagues at *Sowetan*, particularly Chief Photographer Robert Magwaza, Political Editor Mathatha Tsedu, Sports Editor Molefi Mika, Assistant Editor Len Maseko, Night Editor Mike Tissong, sub-editor Zolile Mtshelwane, Assistant News Editor Musa Zondi and Mokgodi Pela. Their ideas and contributions were of great importance. How can I forget the support of former Day Editor Thami Mazwai, now Editor of *Enterprise* magazine, former Managing Editor Moegsien Williams, now editor of the *Cape Times* and former News Editor Sello Rabothata. Finally my gratitude goes to all the *Sowetan* readers who urged me on.

ONE

Gender Equality, Affirmative Action and The New South Africa

Where is Persongaung?

'Mr Herperson Suzperson, chairperson of the Persongaung Civic Association, yesterday charged that policepersons who personned a roadblock outside the township on Friday personhandled their members.' Confused? If you are, then you are sleeping through a revolution. This is the language of the new South Africa where the word 'man' has no place in the dictionaries, newspapers, the Constitution and even the Bible. If you think this is a lot of verbiage, ask the African National Congress. As you may have noticed, they no longer talk about 'one man, one vote'. Instead, they speak of 'one person, one vote'. The word 'man' has not only been declared sexist but taboo. When the ANC was still the government-in-waiting – sorry, that should read the govern(persons)t-in-waiting – its personnel used to work around the clock on new letterheads and stuff for the new Departpersonst of Personpower.

The shadow Minister of Home Affairs was also working behind the scenes, under the instructions of shadow State President Nelson Mandela (oops!!! Persondela), on the study of South African surnames with a view to

1

scrapping sexist ones from the voters' roll. His consultant was Mrs Helen Suzman (it should read Suzperson, you fool) who, during the first plenary session of Codesa, raised the issue of women's participation (or should we say wopersons' participation?) in decision-making structures. The first surname which came under close scrutiny was Younghusband. They said it was a bit sexist but they did not know at the time what they would call the Younghusbands in the new South Africa, although there was a suggestion that they be called Youngpersons. Certain titles that were viewed as sexist in the health sector were also being investigated. One of them was 'midwife'. Now, is the new title going to be 'midperson'?

The million dollar question that is still giving the health workers sleepless nights at ANC headquarters is: what are male nurses who have been elevated to position of sister going to be called in the new South Africa?

Your guess is as good as mine.

God the Mother

Coming back to Mother Earth (is 'Mother' also sexist?), as we always do when we end up confused, priests of the Anglican Church also had problems of their own. After a historic vote in favour of the ordination of women as priests, churchmen (no it should be church-persons) were faced with the question of what to call the new clergy. Bishop Matthew Makhanye of Ladysmith suggested: 'They will have to be called Madams or Madam Reverend but not Father.'

Venerable Victor Spencer of Kimberley disagreed: 'If we are to accept that God the Father also means God the Mother, why shouldn't a lady priest be called Father?'

Dr Mary Jean Silk of Johannesburg added: 'There's nothing wrong with Father. She will belong to a class called Father.'

That's the new South Africa for you.

Here comes Mr Ginwala

Mr Pik Botha, the former Minister of Mineral Affairs, comes across as a very boring and monotonous politician. But he can have a very good sense of humour at times. Allaying fears in Parliament of an impending petrol price increase, Botha tried to be as politically correct and gender sensitive as possible in these changing times. Addressing the new Speaker of Parliament, Dr Frene

Ginwala, Botha said: 'Mr Speaker, the petrol price is dollar driven ...'

Dr Ginwala, who was the first to encourage humour in the new Parliament, was either happy with what she heard or, as one of the foremost engineers of gender equality in this country, felt that addressing a woman (sorry, woperson) as 'Miss', 'Ms' or 'Mrs' was a bit sexist. She would, it appears, rather all mankind (oops, personkind) be referred to as 'Mr'.

Me, I wouldn't mind calling her Mr Ginwala, sir!

Virginal speech

The new Deputy Minister of Provincial Affairs Mr Valli Moosa suggested that there should be no such thing as a maiden speech in the new democratic, non-racial and non-sexist South Africa because maiden was a sexist word. It was on this basis that he refused to make his maiden speech in the new Parliament, preferring instead to call his a 'virginal speech'. Now, since the word 'maiden' is derived from the word 'maid', was Moosa trying to tell us something we didn't know? Was he suggesting that all the maids in Johannesburg's northern suburbs or elsewhere in the country were virgins?

Beware of Wildd women

If acronyms mean what they say, then male chauvinists in South Africa are in for it. Always improperly referred to as members of the 'weaker sex', women have rightly come out smoking in defence of their right to equality.

4

Some time ago a group of women, concerned at their continued ill-treatment by men, came together to form an organisation called People Opposed to Women Abuse whose acronym, Powa, is self-explanatory – women have enormous power in their hands.

Now, those who do not take the acronym (and what it stands for) seriously had better watch out because women are now, it seems, getting wilder and wilder. Otherwise, why would anyone want to start an organisation called Women's Institute for Leadership Development and Democracy which, in short, is known as Wildd?

Equal sex

A few months ago a young white woman drove around the Johannesburg northern suburbs with a bumper sticker reading: 'The more I knew men, the more I loved my dog.' It was there for all to see: this woman was really *gatvol* with male chauvinists and their negative and nasty attitudes towards people of the weaker sex – oops, the 'equal sex'.

But I immediately knew that sooner or later men would respond in their own way. And respond they did. A man was recently spotted driving around the Johannesburg city centre with a bumper sticker reading: 'The more I know of women, the more I like my beer.' Now we know why more and more men are spending most of their time in shebeens and bars these days.

5

It's personmade, not manmade, man!

Poor Dr Piet Koornhof. The more he tries to be politically correct, the more he is out of step with political correctness. Koornhof, by virtue of being associated with the National Party government during the dark days of apartheid, was one of the people who were opposed to mixed marriages. Even though the good ol' doc is now married to Marcel, a coloured woman, it appears he still has a lot of catching up to do. He has shed the stigma of a racist but many people can be excused for thinking he is bloody sexist and a male chauvinist too. During one of Felicia Mabuza-Suttle's *Top Level* programmes, Koornhof confessed that colour was 'a manmade perception'.

Good show, but not good enough.

The word 'manmade', if Koornhof still does not know, should read 'personmade' in the new South Africa.

Men – people of the weaker sex

Just when we thought sexism was out of the window, in comes Lady Margaret Thatcher, former British Prime Minister, who, of all people, should know better. In her controversial memoirs *The Downing Street Years*, published in 1993, the baroness describes men as people of the 'weaker sex'. I suppose that does not only include her husband Denis but also people such as actor Arnold Schwarzenegger, former super middleweight boxer Chris Eubank and Canadian 100 m sprinter Ben Johnson. Still in doubt why they call her the Iron Lady?

One question remains unanswered, though: if men are of the 'weaker sex', are they also of the 'fairer sex'?

People who boil at nothing

Someone claims to have done and completed a scientific study on an 'element' called woman. According to the findings, contained in a pamphlet distributed in the Johannesburg area, the physical properties found in the 'element' called woman are: it boils at nothing; freezes without any known reason; melts if given special treatment and is bitter if incorrectly used. It goes on to say that the 'element' is found in various forms, ranging from virgin metal to common ore. One of the chemical properties, according to the analysis, is that the 'element' is the most powerful money-reducing agent known to man (or should it be person?). It may, the study goes on to say, explode spontaneously without prior warning.

It's not funny, you know.

Felicia Mabuza-Space-Shuttle

I once spoke about birds which were scared of heights. I now know of a woman, a bird if you like, who just loves heights and who can do anything to stay at the top level. She is none other than our own and only high-flying Felicia Mabuza-Suttle who, on her return from the United States a few years ago, perched herself at the top of the SABC's Piet Meyer building in Auckland Park as manager of the corporation's special projects. But this executive producer and presenter of a TV programme

7

that was then aptly titled *Top Level* later realised that Dithering Heights did not go high enough. With the sky as her limit, Mabuza-Suttle has now scaled greater heights. She has packed her bags to join South African Airways as executive manager of corporate relations. As they say, you can't put a good woman down. She has joined a company which will put her where she rightfully belongs: in the air. No wonder they call her Felicia Mabuza-Space-Shuttle.

Executives in the street

'Affirmative action' has become the buzzword of the 90s and a certain company claims to be the leader in this respect, so much so that all its workers, black and white, are in executive positions. Workers who scrub and sweep the floors have been promoted to the position of maintenance executives. Their scooter messenger is now known as a dashing executive. Another company insists on referring to a man who has been working in the mail room for many years as an internal communications consultant rather than a messenger. It has also promoted its 'tea-girl' to the position of beverages manager, complete with a business card. Now, a well-known business scribe who apparently felt some business people were being left behind in the changing world of business, decided that hawkers and fruit and vegetable vendors should be called street executives. This is perhaps a short cut that finally puts them on a par with other business executives such as Raymond Ackerman and Anton Rupert.

Racing against time

We are, as if you were not aware, well into the new South Africa, the land of the Rainbow Nation. But the more we learn to play the new ballgame, the more the past comes back to haunt us. Workers at a leading Johannesburg newspaper company, the one you would think was part of the struggle to rid this country of racial prejudices, were shocked when they received Provident Fund forms recently asking them, among other things, to state their race. Not knowing what to say seeing that we no longer refer to people as white, black or green, one worker filled in the words: horse race. Another simply stated: rat race. If anything, this company is racing against time to become politically correct.

First black nudist

Blacks, who have for a long time been denied equal
opportunities due to apartheid policies, had every
reason to have a feeling of accomplishment every time a
black scored a major first. Over the years, we have had
the first black chartered accountant, the first black civil
engineer, the first black clinical psychologist and the first
black nuclear scientist, to mention but a few.

A hack at a Sunday newspaper had every reason to be
overjoyed, I suppose, when he became the first black
person to appear in the nude at South Africa's only
nudist resort, the Beau Valley Country Club near
Warmbaths, a previously whites only resort. What's
more, the journalist even posed for a picture – in the
nude – and held hands with nudist and owner of the

resort, Beau Brummel, who had caused a stir several months earlier when he had streaked across a rugby field. With a black streaker in our midst, soccer matches at FNB Stadium will no longer be a big yawn. Go for it, my man.

Where is the black Joe Soap?

The former chairman of the Constitutional Assembly and General Secretary of the African National Congress, Mr Cyril Ramaphosa, was pleasantly surprised the other day when *Sowetan* Political Editor Mathatha Tsedu referred, during a TV debate on the drafting of the Constitution, to what you would call the man in the street as Joe Soap. Ramaphosa was probably right to show his surprise because in South Africa the man in the street, in terms of the demographic situation and social realities, is usually a black person who wouldn't have a name and surname like that. Tsedu was quick to see Ramaphosa's point and did not make the same mistake the second time around when he spoke on the same subject.

This time he came up with the black equivalent of Joe Soap. He called him Sipho Gumede. But Sipho Gumede is not a man in the street. He is one of South Africa's gifted musicians who must have been amused when he heard his name mentioned on the programme. But there is indeed a black Joe Soap out there. Would he please stand up?

My friend, the petrol attendant

Petrol attendants are, to many people, individuals whose usefulness is limited to filling our tanks, checking the oil and cleaning the windscreen. But a well-known black Johannesburg journo has now learned to respect and like them for what they are.

The other day the newsman, who lives in a historically white suburb, was getting ready to attend a glittering, not-to-be-missed black tie function in the city when he couldn't find his bow-tie. He turned his bedroom upside down but could not find the bow-tie, which was effectively the ticket to the function.

A drive to Soweto, where he had hoped to get one from friends, did not yield the desired results. Dejected and frustrated, the journalist drove back to his suburban home when, all of a sudden, an idea struck him. Quickly he drove to a filling station near his home where, guess what, all the petrol attendants wore bow-ties. Fishing a R20 note out of his back pocket, the journalist succeeded in negotiating with one of the petrol attendants, who agreed to lend him his bow-tie for a few hours as he was about to knock off anyway.

Moral of the story? Don't look down on your brothers when you are on your way up as you may need them on your way down.

Caught with their pants down – literally

Gender equality has been on everyone's lips these days, especially after women from across the world converged in Beijing, China, in 1995 to shape their future. In South Africa, however, women have a tendency of taking gender equality a little bit too far – sometimes into the loo.

At a jazz concert in Heidelberg, where the waters of immortality were available in liberal quantities, some women did something that had never been done before. When the time came for them to answer the call of nature, they made a beeline to the ladies' toilets. When they found them totally inadequate, they unilaterally decided to storm the gents' toilets where they caught many of the men with their pants down, literally speaking.

He's my loving bantoe boyfriend

An adventurous young black journo put the Rainbow Nation to the test the other day when he went down to the Cape Peninsula on a job. On arrival, our bright-eyed journalist decided he wanted a female companion to keep him company for the duration of his stay. It was not long before he fell for a coloured woman who, in turn, did not hesitate to return his love. As the two were getting to know each other better between the sheets, the young girl confessed to the journo: 'You know, it's the first time in my life that I've done it with a *bantoe*.'

The confession hit the poor fellow like a ton of bricks but he tried very hard to suppress his anger. He knew that if he did not keep a firm grip on his temper, he would spoil his adventure and would never see this naïve but stunningly gorgeous young coloured lady again.

The next day the journalist left his hotel room in the city to visit his lover at her Mitchell's Plain home as had earlier been arranged. When he rang the doorbell, a younger girl came to the door and opened it. She gave him one lazy look and without saying a word to him turned and called into the house: 'Charmaine, your *bantoe* boyfriend is here.'

It then occurred to him that at the time the Western Cape was still NP country where not everyone had crossed the Rubicon into the new South Africa.

Gravy train goes to prison

The news of the goods-laden gravy train has seemingly spread to all corners of South Africa, even to our prisons. An ambitious prisoner at Barberton Prison, in response to an advertisement, applied for a job as a sub-editor at a leading Johannesburg newspaper the other day. Although his qualifications and skills did not even begin to meet the newspaper's requirements, the prisoner was overly optimistic of striking it rich once he got the job. In his CV, the prisoner did not forget to mention that his favourite car was a Toyota Camry. Someone must have forgotten to tell him that the gravy train is so fast that very few journalists have been able to board it.

Time to act on sexist Germany

When the anti-sexist lobby says it wants to rewrite history, don't underestimate its efforts. Even certain sections of the Church have agreed that the Bible is a sexist document which needs to be revised. The lobby, however, has not said a single word about Germany. As far as I'm concerned, Germany is still discriminating against people on the basis of sex. If it wasn't, it wouldn't be calling its citizens Germans. There are women living there too, you know. So until the country changes its name to Gerpersony and its citizens are known as Gerpersons, it can be maintained that Germany is a sexist country.

You make my heart sing

A Government announcement that sex discrimination was unlawful and unconstitutional was probably silently received with a pinch of salt by hardened male chauvinists. But they can rest assured that there is really nothing to fear. With the bad news, if you can call it that, comes the good news. You see, it is no longer taboo or embarrassing for a woman to propose love to a man. If you don't believe me, here's an example.

A young journalist on a Johannesburg morning newspaper fell in love with her new boss the very first week he arrived. Not quite sure how to express her feelings face to face with him, the happy-go-lucky reporter ended up placing a Valentine message in the smalls section of the newspaper.

She wrote: 'My heart has been aflame since you came as a surprise. You opened my eyes. Every time you say: "Hey," my nerves go astray. I lose my ways. Your sexy voice shivers down my livers. See if you can guess.'

Unfortunately the poor fellow never got round to knowing who the writer was.

Scoring a point

A diehard soccer fan who watched the World Cup qualifier between South Africa and Angola on TV took twenty minutes to realise it wasn't Bafana Bafana who were mesmerising the Angolans on the field. He only realised it was South Africa's women's soccer squad he was watching after Anna Monate scored the first goal and her name was flashed across the TV screen. This is either a compliment for Sandile Bali, coach of the South African women's soccer squad, or a serious indictment on the quality of soccer played by national soccer coach Clive Barker's boys. Whichever way you look at it, people who say there must be gender equality in South Africa have a point.

TWO

Names and Places

My name is Perpetual

Christening a newly born baby in any community is one of those rare moments which many parents cherish. In the black community it has become an art through which parents express their innermost feelings about life, its ups and downs, their hopes and their fears, their frustrations and their wishes. The colonisation of the African continent, which brought with it a lot of Western values and influences, has also left an indelible legacy as many parents try to upstage and outclass one another by giving their babies 'unique' and 'very fancy English' names. A glance through the 1994 black Matric results provided an insight into the thinking behind the christening of a child.

To many parents names such as Mary, John or David are in this day and age too common and too primitive to be given to their children who they rightly consider to be very special people who deserve to be bestowed with very special names. While names such as Honey, Prosperous, Progress, Precious, Perseverance, Perfectionist, Pleasant, Pleasure, Consolation, Confidence, Sweetness, Goodness and Success are no longer new in the christening vocabulary, some parents these days go for 'unusual and special' names such as Republic, Fiddle, Remember, Active, Pardon, Perpetual, Addition and Lifebuoy.

There are, as we speak, girls who are called Victress which, I suspect, is the female version of Victor and a fancier name than the already tired and over-used Victoria.

While the names Gift and Given are self-explanatory, I'm still battling to find the meaning of Giftless and Gifter. Gifter, I suppose, is someone who gives. As for Giftless, your guess is as good as mine. Many parents wish to see their children grow to become very important and educated people in society. That's perhaps why we find people with names such as Doctor, Nurse, Captain, Advocate, Deacon, Navigator and Director in our midst. How nice it would be to have a doctor called Dr Doctor Khumalo or an army captain known as Captain Captain Khorombi. Then there are parents who, for some strange reason, want to hide the meaning of their offsprings' names. After paging through a number of English dictionaries, I still have to find the meaning of names such as Decreasious, Duracious, Herbsiveamount, Carefulling and Eusenthium. What still puzzles me, though, is why would one call his or her newly born baby Necessary, Question, Reason or Wireless?

This happens when whites, the people blacks are supposedly trying to emulate, still christen their children simply as Mary-Jane, William, Grant or Edward. As for me I still love names such as Thivhudziswi, Sizwe and

19

Lerato. They are simple, straightforward, rich in meaning and have a ring of Africanness about them.

Going MAD in a hostel

They don't know it but when the licensing department in Pretoria introduced the computer-based number plates a few years ago they averted what could have become a chaotic situation of unimaginable proportions in the violent months leading up to the country's first democratic elections.

As you may have observed, most of the number plates do not have vowels, otherwise we would today find ourselves with number plates reading something like this: 'MAD 111T' or 'DOM 323T'. Just imagine what people's reaction would be if ANC's Thabo Mbeki were to be seen driving around in a car with a registration number 'IFP 007'!

During those violent days, anyone alighting from a car bearing registration number 'ANC 747' or 'PAC 404T' at a Reef hostel would be dead meat. It would also be very uncomfortable for anyone driving a car with registration WAR 543T as people would think he was a warmonger or warlord who would be quick to draw his guns at the slightest provocation. It would be equally embarrassing to be seen driving around in a jalopy with the registration BUM 444T distinctly displayed at the back and front.

But just imagine what people's reaction would be if a motorist were to be seen driving through a busy city street in a car with the registration SPY 001T conspicuously displayed at the rear and front of the car. I bet you that even though we have just emerged from the dark days of apartheid, that person would be eaten alive.

However, I suppose it is not worse than to be seen driving a car with registration RIP 777T. A car with a registration like that would obviously be regarded as a mobile coffin.

SEX and my number plate

It is not too hard to find why Gauteng wants to allow motorists in the region to use personalised number plates from now on. People such as MEC for housing Dan Mofokeng and his safety and security counterpart Jessie Duarte have vested interests in this and want

people to recognise them immediately wherever they go. So in future when you see a top of the range BMW bearing this number plate: DAN 737 GP, you must know it belongs to no one else but the honourable comrade Dan Mofokeng.

You won't mistake comrade Jessie Duarte's car because it will carry a number plate like this: JES 320 GP. Premier Tokyo Sexwale, we are told, is also seriously considering using a personalised number plate on his official vehicle. His will almost certainly look like this: SEX 733 GP. . .

Ons is nie moegoes nie

We know now why the licensing authorities in Gauteng did not want to use the first three letters in Gauteng – GAU or gau – in their new number plates. Gau, for those who do not know, is a *tsotsi taal* word for an academically challenged person, *moegoe* or, if you like, a Jim-comes-to-Gauteng type of a person. You see, people living in Gauteng are perceived to be cleverer than *plaasjapies* and would hate you forever if you were to refer to them as *Magau*.

Following in Mangope's footsteps

Northern Province Premier Ngoako Ramatlhodi seems to be following in the footsteps of former Bophuthatswana president Chief Lucas Mangope, even though he did not like him one bit during the apartheid era. Mangope, many people will remember, regarded the Bophuthatswana bantustan and everything in it as his personal possessions. He was on many occasions heard to say: '*Ke stadiyami samme*' (It's my stadium), '*ke batho bamme*' (it's my people), '*ke univesithi yamme*' (it's my university) and so on and so forth.

Now, in the Northern Province, there are so many number plates that start with the letters BBR that questions have started being raised. People living there say, however, that these number plates either stand for *Batho Ba Rona* (Our People) or *Batho Ba Ramatlhodi* (Ramatlhodi's People).

Now, do I hear the honourable Premier saying: 'If Mangope did it, why can't I *did* it too?'

University known as Rauteng

The Rand Afrikaanse Universiteit, RAU in short, is among many educational institutions which during the apartheid era helped perpetuate the policy of separate development by refusing to admit students of colour to their campuses. RAU was also there to maintain and promote the selfish and narrow interests of the Afrikaner and his policies. But now that the tables have turned, RAU can be commended for having made some visible strides in trying to keep pace with the sweeping changes taking place across the country.

However, the changes have not gone far enough. The university must, among other things, also change its name if it wants to completely shed its baggage of the past.

Can we suggest that the institution from now on be called Rauteng?

Welcome to Maharajstad

For the new South Africa to be really meaningful, part of our past has, fortunately or unfortunately, got to die. This includes everything that has been associated with racism, apartheid and colonialism, such as names given to historic buildings, streets, towns and cities that we have taken for granted for a long time. The first name that must really get the chop is Ventersdorp, home to Afrikaner Weerstandsbeweging leader Eugéne Terre'Blanche. The neo-fascist leader can rant and rave until he is blue in the face but the town will have to be renamed in the new South Africa. It will probably soon be known as Maharajstad, in honour of the contributions made towards liberation by African National Congress executive member Mac Maharaj.

Mmabatho, that town in Bophuthatswana that has always been Chief Lucas Mangope's personal property, will, in all probability, be known as Popo's Haven or Molefe's Retreat since Mangope's fantasy in Bophuthatswana has come to an end.

When it comes to street names, Kaptein Street in Hillbrow, Johannesburg, somehow immediately comes to mind. This is probably because it reminds one of the ruthlessness with which white police captains interrogated opponents of apartheid during the dark days of separate development. Since young lovers like to take their nightly strolls in this street, would it not be appropriate to rename it Lovers' Lane? But to be seen to be politically correct, we can also call it the Tokyo Sexwale Drive (no prefixes please!). But if all these places and streets have to be renamed, so does John Vorster Square, a police station notorious for deaths in detention, torture and other human rights abuses, named after one of the most *verkrampte* prime ministers South Africa has ever had.

Are there any takers from the ANC?

My friend is a dog

A youth columnist once described a friend as someone you always have fun with. Now a certain guy known as Ginger Mabasa also has lots and lots of buddies who give him a pat on the back whenever he does something out of the ordinary. What beats me is that his friends call him *Inja*, Zulu for dog. The name has stuck like glue.

With friends like these, who needs enemies? It should, however, be comforting for Mabasa to know he is not the first person to go by the name of *Inja*. A few years ago the then American Secretary of State Henry Kissinger visited these shores in an attempt to sell the American policy. Disenfranchised and vote-less South Africans were not amused, and told him to pack and go. But not before they had nicknamed him 'Kiss Inja'. The difference here is that the honourable former Secretary of State was regarded more as a foe than a friend.

Prison called Lost City

Someone at the Department of Correctional Services has a score to settle with Sol Kerzner. In fact, he's out to match the hotel magnate brick for brick. The mortar had hardly dried at Sun City, Sol's imposing entertainment complex in what is now known as the North West region, when the gentleman at Correctional Services also decided that Sun City would be a perfect name for Diepkloof Prison. Sol went a step further when he built the Lost City. But he could not outwit his opponent, who moved swiftly to announce that the Boksburg Prison was now unofficially known as Lost City. The prison, ironically, lay vacant for several months – lost to the growing prison population.

Masondo's crooked wheels

Gauteng MEC for health, Mr Amos Masondo, must be regretting the day he became part of the Masondo clan.

Amasondo is a Zulu word for 'wheels'. This name has been following and haunting him ever since he found himself behind the steering wheel of the health sector in the region. The sector is always plagued by strikes, theft of medicines and linen, corruption and general discontent. And the blame is put squarely on his shoulders all the time. So, instead of finding himself like the other politicians on the gravy train whose wheels are smooth and well oiled, Masondo is still driving his rickety and over-used jalopy with wheels which can come off anytime.

IFP = Indignant, Filibustering, Problematic

Inkatha Freedom Party president Chief Mangosuthu Buthelezi says the abbreviation IFP stands for Integrity, Freedom and Progress or 'I'm For Peace'. The good ol' chief is probably right. But he appears to have conveniently and intentionally forgotten that Inkatha to many people means *inkathazo* (trouble maker). That's why some people say IFP actually stands for Indignant, Filibustering and Problematic.

Geewuz, all these men are boys

President Nelson Mandela, who once called on all South Africans never again to refer to an adult male as a 'boy', may succeed where others have failed – to change the nickname of our national soccer squad. If the president has his way, many people I know will have to make an appointment with the Minister of Home Affairs, Chief Mangosuthu Buthelezi, because they will need the names that appear in their IDs changed to conform with the changing times. Yes, they will go to him, cap in hand, because he is the only person who has an authority to make alterations in their IDs. This they will do whether they like it or not. The first person whose name readily comes to mind is Bafana Khumalo, the once-dreadlocked former *Mail & Guardian* columnist who, I'm sure, also hates to go by the name 'Boys', because that's precisely what his name means. If Khumalo feels jittery about facing the chief alone, he will have to rope in his namesake at *The Star*, Bafana Shezi who, I'm quite cer-

27

tain, will feel secure only if the team is strengthened by a third person.

They will have quite a few options. One, former National Soccer League's Public Relations Officer, Fanyana Shiburi, is not only Shezi's contact but he is just a phone call away. Shezi may even know where to get hold of Boy George Mashinini, a very ambitious photographer who used to freelance for *The Star*. Shiburi may contribute in strengthening the group by bringing in his own namesakes, educationist Fanyana Mazibuko and former boxer Fanyana Sidumo, and show the chief that they are, contrary to what their names suggest, not 'small boys'. The SABC is also not in short supply of 'boys'. Perched on top of the list are actors Boykie Motlhamme and Boykie Phoolo. Their team is strengthened by Boiki Mothei, a former *City Press* sports writer who is now working in the publicity department of SABC 1. Geewuz, I didn't know we had so many 'boys' in the entertainment and communications world.

Anyway, good luck guys. Or is it boys?

Unpoetic, tongue-twisting names

Tongue-twisting double-barrelled surnames, if that's the word, are becoming a common feature we'll have to live with in these fast changing times. While I have nothing against people with twin surnames, I particularly find them unnecessary. People have to go to extreme, painful lengths to try to pronounce these names, wasting valuable time in the process. In these times, every second counts. A fourteen character surname like

28

Tlhotlhalemaje (with apologies to my favourite DJ Cocky 'Two Bull') is long enough, poetic and acceptable. But the tongue begins to lose its rhythm when it has to deal with a name like Dr Mary-Jane Myakayaka-Tlhotlhalemaje. It is even worse when one of the names is African and the other German, British or Bosnian.

Worthless coin(incidence)

When South Africa did away with the R2 note and introduced the R2 coin in its place in the early 90s, it did not take long before the coin was called a 'De Klerk'. This was apparently because its introduction coincided with the bold reform initiatives that were spearheaded by the then State President F W de Klerk. Now that the coin features the Xhosa language, the continued use of F W's name in reference to the coin has begun to have no relevance at all. Maybe the new coin should be named after Xhosa-speaking and ageing Eastern Cape Premier Raymond Mhlaba. After all, the R2 coin is becoming more worthless by the day.

Satanic Verses

Next time you see a bumper sticker with the words 'My name is Driew', steer clear of the man behind the wheel. He could be a Satanist. Spelt backwards, the word Driew reads 'weird'. Members of the Satanic cult, who are threatening to change the course of civilisation in South Africa and the rest of the world, have this strange tendency of doing things backwards. While everybody else tries to move forward, they want to take us backwards. A journalist recently saw the words 'I love Natasha' sprayed on a dilapidated house occupied by a group of Satanists in a Johannesburg suburb. The 'Natasha' mentioned in the graffiti was neither a girl nor a woman. When the first five letters are spelt backwards they read: Satan.

Now, anyone who publicly declares his or her love for Satan clearly needs their head examined. Then there was this weird guy, with bizarre tattoos and always in black, who used to operate a fly-by-night financial concern called Reficul in the Johannesburg city centre. Again, when the name is spelt backwards, it reads: Lucifer.

God save us from these Satanic Verses.

A mango called Mangosuthu

President Nelson Mandela, F W de Klerk and Home Affairs Minister Chief Mangosuthu Buthelezi are three of the most talked about political figures in South Africa today. They have travelled the length and breadth of the globe and their achievements and actions have made them three of the best known South African political personalities in the world. But my personal computer, a very intelligent and sophisticated piece of equipment which can solve a complicated mathematical problem in a split second or make someone dance on the ceiling, thinks otherwise.

In fact, it has never heard of a man called Mandela. The closest its spell function can get is Candela, described by the Collins Dictionary and Thesaurus as

the basic SI unit of luminous intensity, or the intensity, in a perpendicular direction, of a surface of 1/600 000 square metres of a black body at the temperature of freezing platinum under a pressure of 101 325 a square metre. What a mouthful!

As for De Klerk, my PC reckons he is one of the clerks we see working behind a worn out desk at the post office. It does not occur to it that he once ran this country.

It knows who Bill Clinton is, but it hasn't heard of a Buthelezi or a Mangosuthu either. In fact it confuses Mangosuthu with a mango.

So, what more can the three gentlemen really do to earn recognition from this little piece of equipment? They, however, should not lose heart – it doesn't recognise Boris Yeltsin either. After all, he too is not an American.

Poles and Holes

What do you call people who come from Holland? Hollanders, perhaps? Yes, but there is an argument that if we can call people who come from Poland Poles, we should as well call those from Holland Holes.

GNU = Great National Uncertainty

South Africans are so much in love with coining new acronyms that it has become a national pastime. We have had Soweto, Codesa, Sadtu, Satdu, Cosag, TEC, to name just a few. One of the surprise additions in this ever growing list of acronyms is GNU. The New Collins

Dictionary says a gnu is 'either of two sturdy antelopes inhabiting the savannas of Africa, having an oxlike head and a long tufted tail. Also *wildebeest* (wild beast).' But, as it also turns out, GNU stands for the Government of National Unity – the government that will rule this country until 1999. Some people, however, describe GNU as the Great National Uncertainty. With a lot of uncertainty brewing in the air, who can blame them?

Biting the hand that feeds you

A name is the single most important possession a man can ever have. But some of our white compatriots have scant regard for black people's names. Soccer referee Ian McLeod is one example. The controversial whistleman can't spell the name Kgomotso Modise even though as chief of the National Soccer League Modise used to pay his salary at the end of the day. In a report he compiled for the league the other day, the closest McLeod could get in spelling Modise was 'Modese'. Not only that, but he referred to former Orlando Pirates coach Phil 'Jones' Setshedi as Phil Ntsedi.

I suppose the diminutive referee would not mind if people started calling him Iron McCloud even though his hand is made of clay.

Sir, your name is weird

After a certain radio station inadvertently, or otherwise, called Conservative Party leader Ferdi Hartzenberg, Herdi Fartzenberg, the SABC had to move swiftly to repair the damage. Hartzenberg had every reason to become hot under the collar. Like I say above, the single most important and precious thing a person can ever possess is his or her name. Any distortion or omission to a name is not only an insult but it strips you of your pride, your dignity and your identity. Dr Hartzenberg, however, is not the only person to have been humiliated in this way. I, for instance, have been called all sorts of names, if you can excuse the pun, so many times that I'm no longer sure if my dignity is still intact. The names range from Makaranga to Makhareng. Some apparently mistake me for a black Scotsman and call me McRing. But the one that obviously takes the cake is Make-A-Ring. Some people even go to the extent of saying my surname is weird.

Forewarned is forearmed

Someone has a premonition that the former Venda homeland is about to be struck by a disaster of immeasurable magnitude. Writing in *Thohoyandou News*, the unidentified man says, and I quote (verbatim): 'As elsewhere in the world, the risk of disaster is seen to increase with population growth. Here in Venda people are building allover even along and in the valley. At this pointing time we are not realising the danger of floods. The time will come, and it is already here summer season. I advise you to recognize flooding as a potential disaster at those area. As such, I also extend my appeal to you to take preventative steps before the actual flood sweeps your homes away. Please, take these advise seriously in order to survive all consequences on any disaster.'

Don't say you were not warned.

Chickens have come home to roost, F W

In KwaZulu-Natal a visiting head of state from any-where in the world would be given a traditional weapon as a gift, not only as a gesture of goodwill but also as an arrogant show of strength. In the former Gazankulu homeland, the gift would take the form of *timbila* (an African piano), while in Lesotho and the Free State you can bet your bottom dollar that the present would either be a *seanamarena* blanket or a *mokorokotlo* hat.

But in Soweto, a multilingual and multicultural society, anything is possible. In fact, the gift would depend on the mood of the people and the message they would like to convey to the recipient at that very moment. So there was more to it than met the eye when the then State President F W de Klerk was presented with a live chicken during his 1994 election trail in the sprawling township. The message behind the gift was crystal clear: for you to have visited Soweto after all these years the chickens must have come home to roost. The gift was also apparently meant to warn De Klerk that unless he did something dramatic, his National Party would become chicken feed at the April 27, 1994 polls. And that is exactly what happened. Before he chickened out of Soweto after discovering he had over-stayed his visit, a fruit and vegetable vendor gave him another gift – an apple. The message behind the apple? An apple a day keeps a De Klerk away.

Queen Motlepula, Mr P W Ngwenya and Cheeskop

Deputy President Thabo Mbeki's christening of the Queen of England as Motlalepula – the one who brings rain – is to be welcomed. But, as the honourable Comrade Mbeki knows, charity should have begun at home. There is a feeling in some quarters that the Deputy President should have considered fellow countrymen and women first before giving an African name to a foreigner such as Her Majesty the Queen.

It is felt that the first person who should have been considered for this honourable gesture is former State President P W Botha, whose iron-fisted rule earned him the nickname *Groot Krokodil*. It is perhaps high time in the new South Africa to start calling the former head of state Mr P W Ngwenya because that is precisely what *krokodil* is in Zulu.

Then there is F W de Klerk, whose bald head has become his trademark wherever he goes. The Zulu name for anyone who is bald-headed is Mpandlane, a name that would fit our beloved F W like a glove. Comrade Mbeki could have even gone a step further and called his former colleague in the Government of National Unity Cheeskop, the *tsotsi taal* version of Mpandlane.

I cannot think of any African name that would fit Rowan Cronje other than Mahambehlala (one who is always on the move). For after fleeing the advent of democracy in Zimbabwe, Cronje found himself in Ciskei. When the heat eventually became unbearable for him there, he fled to Bophuthatswana where he became Chief Lucas Mangope's blue-eyed boy. When Mangope's reign came to an abrupt end, Cronje bolted out and no one seems to know where he is right now.

Is it therefore wrong to say Cronje's African name should be Mahambehlala?

Stooping too low?

While there are people who try to live up to what their names mean, there are those who simply try to do the opposite. One of such people is Lucus Stoop, acting director general of the Public Service Commission. Stoop once turned down proposals of a special pay deal for the

Department of Inland Revenue that was aimed at ending the brain drain of experienced tax collectors. Ms Gill Marcus, then chairperson of the standing committee on finance, also failed to convince Stoop that the deal would be in the best interests of the Government. It was clear that Stoop did not want to be seen to be stooping too low.

Save his Bacon

We're reliably told that Peter Bacon, boss of Sun International, does not consider his breakfast complete if it does not include bacon and eggs. And what's more, as a successful businessman, Mr Bacon knows that at the end of the day he has got to bring the bacon home.

Place of kings

One of the most important things to have happened in this part of the world has been the correction of mistakes created by years of colonialism. Do you still remember the time when they used to call Botswana the Bechuanaland Protectorate, and Lesotho the Basotholand Protectorate? Some time ago South African maps showed a place called Mafeking. Someone – I'm not sure if it was Chief Lucas Mangope – spotted the mistake and it was duly corrected.

The place today is known by its rightful name: Mafikeng – the place of rocks. Maybe the colonialists thought it was a place of kings, who knows?

Suing Suzanne

A male journalist on a certain Sunday newspaper was baffled and embarrassed when his colleagues started calling him Suzanne. The journalist spent several sleepless nights trying to figure out if he had somehow just become a victim of gender equality. Try as he did he could not come up with an answer. Well, a highly placed and extremely reliable source at the newspaper has thrown some light on the issue. He says the name originated from the word 'sue', which is not only short for Suzanne but which also means 'to institute legal action'.

My impeccable source said the newspaper had received so many letters from lawyers threatening to sue the journalist for the sensational and unsubstantiated stories he wrote for the publication that it had become clear that some of his 'exclusives' had been sucked from his thumb. The flood of letters continued to pour into the editor's office until his colleagues decided to do something about it. So they called him Suzanne, or Sue, if you like.

A veXing question of X's name

When former Pan Africanist Congress general secretary Benny AleXander dropped his 'slave name' and opted for !Khoisan X, he gave us a longwinded, incomprehensible and confusing Xplanation as to why he was doing it. We can now, however, reveal that his Xtraordinary decision, if you like, had more to do with his religious beliefs than the historical background he cited in his paper.

It had nothing to do with his obsession for the *X-Files*, a TV drama series that had him glued to the screen for Xtended periods every time it was screened. Neither did it have anything to do with the number of Xs he saw when South Africans went to the polls to elect a new democratic government on April 27, 1994.

You see, !Khoisan X, a direct descendant of the great prophet !Jesus X, was chosen by his gods to rescue their religion, Xianity, from Xtinction. As a staunch and committed member of Xianity, !Khoisan X is an Xian, just as believers of Christianity are called Christians. !Jesus X was born on the same day as Jesus Christ, December 25. But unlike Jesus Christ who was crucified, !Jesus X was aXed to death coincidentally on the same day. Even though !Jesus X's death did not get the blaze of publicity that Jesus Christ's received, his religion and legacy continued to flourish, albeit underground. That's why when Christians today celebrate Christmas in honour of their Lord, !Khoisan X, fellow Xians and other Xponents of Xianity and its Xtended family gather to wish one another a happy Xmas and indulge in Xtra merry-making.

Immobilised by the big toe

Many reasons have been advanced as to why big international corporations are reluctant to invest in Gauteng even though the province is the powerhouse of the South African economy. Some say the spiralling crime rate, especially the alarming increase in car hijackings, has helped to harden business attitudes against South Africa. Others still cite laziness and perceived low productivity levels among blacks, the significant workforce in terms of numbers, as the reason for this lack of business interest in Gauteng. The perceptions are, of course, way off the mark. People in the know say the real reason for the 'hands off Gauteng' attitude is because the region has the biggest prevalence of *gout*. Gout is defined by the New Collins Dictionary as a metabolic disease characterised by painful inflammation of certain joints, especially the big toe, caused by deposits of sodium urate. Because of this, the disease has an immobilising effect on the workforce, especially on Mondays. That's why Gauteng is sometimes known as *Gouteng*.

What a Mutual partner

What's in a name? Well, quite a lot, especially if you are in the insurance industry. I bet the captains of the industry were not amused when they saw a pamphlet that has been circulating in the streets of Johannesburg for some time now. The pamphlet reads:

'If you sleep with your wife, that's Legal and General but if you sleep with someone else, it is Mutual and Federal.

'If you sleep with your mother-in-law, that's Old Mutual and if you sleep with a prostitute, that's a Commercial Union.

'If you sleep with everyone in Africa, that's African Life but if your wife allows you to sleep around, it's called Liberty Life.'

One wonders how many people do it the Old Mutual way.

Viva Fivaz Viva

Many people still do not know why national Police Commissioner George Fivaz landed the plummest police job in the country after the April 27, 1994 general elections. Well, it is true that his impressive curriculum vitae and his colourful police record could have, to a certain extent, played a part. But there is a school of thought that suggests that Fivaz got the nod from the Minister of Safety and Security, Mr Sydney Mufamadi, because of his seemingly politically correct name. The name, somehow associated with the sloganeering that helped bring down the apartheid regime, sounded like music to the minister's ears. That's perhaps why in the townships some people pronounce it as 'Vivas'.

This man is worth Half-a-G

People of Indian descent are always, rightly or otherwise, associated with riches. But when a relatively unknown Indian chap stood as a candidate for the African National Congress in the November 1, 1995 local government elections in Roodepoort, his fate had already been sealed. No one wanted to touch him and the poor man went on to lose the elections. The reason?

His name is Yusuf Haffejee. In some quarters Haffejee is pronounced as Half-a-G, short for half-a-grand or R500. Indeed, who would vote for a person who has only R500 in the kitty?

Once a Gautengese . . .

The disgraced former MEC for agriculture in the North West, Rocky Malebane-Metsing, was probably right after all: Premier Popo Molefe is a Gautengese through and through. When the Premier needed treatment for his diabetes, he went all the way to the Brenthurst Clinic, right in the heart of Gauteng and a few kilometres from his Alexandra Township home, even though there are hospitals in the North West. So don't be surprised if the North West Premier says to you: 'Don't ask me about the North West, I just work there.' As they say, you can take Molefe out of Gauteng but you cannot take Gauteng out of Molefe.

UDF alive, well and kicking

The United Democratic Front (UDF) is dead and buried but its memories will live with us for many years to come. At the height of the internecine violence in the mid-80s, many people suspected to be traitors, informers or reactionaries were executed by the terrifying 'necklace' method. Many of these executions, which entailed placing a burning tyre around the victim's neck, were wrongly or otherwise attributed to members of the

43

UDF. UDF, its detractors said, stood for 'Uniroyal, Dunlop and Firestone' – all of which are names of tyres.

In Giyani, the capital town of the former Gazankulu homeland, UDF is now the name of a section of the township inhabited mainly by single women. According to the sources in the township, the abbreviation UDF stands for 'Unmarried, Divorced and Frustrated'.

Long live UDF, long live.

Chris is on the Ball at last . . .

President Nelson Mandela says in his autobiography *Long Walk to Freedom* that names do not necessarily shape the destiny of those to whom they are given. But the President should know better because if he had not lived up to his name Rolihlahla (Xhosa for trouble-stirrer), we would probably not be where we are today, politically speaking.

A name that clearly demonstrates that names can shape your destiny is that of Chris Ball, former managing director of First National Bank. Ball was not exactly having a ball – that's probably why he resigned – at First National Bank. What with a controversy surrounding him, Mrs Winnie Mandela and the now defunct United Democratic Front over a loan involving thousands of rands. He went overseas but was apparently not exactly happy there, and came back. Now Ball is seemingly on the ball as the driving force behind the committee that is organising Cape Town's bid for the year 2004 Olympic Games.

The ball is in your court, Chris. Keep it rolling.

... and Bath is having a bath

Then there is Vincent Bath, a spokesman for Rand Water (formerly Rand Water Board), which at some stage faced a seemingly insurmountable water crisis. As you cannot have a bath if the bath is not filled with water, Vincent Bath can't make a living if there is a water shortage in the country.

Eager to probe cops ...

Transparency is one of the buzzwords that have taken the new South Africa by storm. The word is not only on everyone's lips but has firmly taken root even in the police force, once perceived as the custodians of apartheid policies. This is especially because the then South African police force was always accused of covering up every time police officers had to investigate other police officers. To show that the new South African Police Service has taken the lead in the transparency stakes, it makes it a point that it appoints police officers with appropriate names to investigate other police officers. Like Adriaan Eager who was appointed to investigate the killing by a policeman of serial killer suspect David Selepe. No one appeared to be too eager to tackle this one except Eager. Let's hope the new South Africa will produce more eager policemen like Eager.

... Now here comes a Grave problem

While the South African Police Service has Adriaan Eager, Sky Television News has its own Keith Graves.

Graves, the network's correspondent in the war-ravaged parts of the Middle East, spells death wherever he goes. It seems people in the Middle East start digging graves in anticipation of more deaths whenever they see Graves pitching his tent in their neighbourhood.

Watch out for these cereal killers

Professor Mohale Mahanyele, chairman of the beleaguered National Sorghum Breweries, must be cursing the day his marketing department decided to use the word *iyavaya* (*tsotsi taal* for 'it goes down well') to promote its first clear beer product, Vivo Fine Lager. Mahanyele now says the reason the product is going down the drain instead of down consumers' throats is that the concept adopted by his marketing department suggests that the lager is brewed by people with gangster or *tsotsi* mentality.

Perhaps Mahanyele is also trying to tell us that he thinks Radio 702, Gauteng's leading talk radio station, is run and managed by people with gangster mentality. Who can blame the good ol' prof? He must have seen a couple of billboards around Gauteng which, among others, read: 'Hola magents' and 'Heyta Gauteng', both *tsotsi taal* ways of greeting. His thinking is perhaps cemented by the fact that John Robbie and Dan Moyane, who host the breakfast slot, are called 'cereal killers'.

THREE

Politics

Politically correct stealing

As South Africans start getting used to the new South Africa, people will, it appears, have to familiarise themselves with the new politically correct terminology that comes with it. The words 'theft' and 'steal' are soon to disappear from our dictionaries as any action that would normally be perceived as theft is now considered as 'affirmative redistribution', especially if the victim is white or a member of the so-called black middle class. The toyi-toyi, which was very popular during the dark days of apartheid but which is now apparently on the way out since President Nelson Mandela sounded the death knell on mass action, is now widely known as 'industrial aerobics'.

Funny galore

When our leaders took a decision at the World Trade Centre in Kempton Park that South Africa should have eleven official languages, they meant just that. There are, however, people who have interpreted the decision to mean that, for practical and logistical considerations, all eleven languages should be merged into one official pidgin.

47

These people have already started to converse with fellow South Africans in that language with, I'm afraid to say, very discouraging results. They first tried to create awareness of this 'new official language' through the wire service of the South African Press Association. But no one could apparently grasp what they wanted to convey. Below is an example of how they want the 'new official language' to sound:

JOHANNESBURG - InWaxha Free/m Parhy leades Mangosuthu Buthelezi on Thursday 3aid armud insurrection in KwaZulu/Natal was not a possiblalmty, gven if people expected itpo@happen. SpeaSing at a Pruss briefing iN Johannesburg, Mr buthulezi said mt would be sad if Souph Africa moved in that directyon.
@ASKED WHATHE W+ = '

Come to think of it, wouldn't life be much easier if we were to have an official language like this? After all, we already have Fanagalo.

Come inside, chief

Talking about the 'possiblalmtym of armud insurrection', we have never doubted – despite the filibustering and the shifting of goalposts – that Inkatha Freedom Party leader Chief Mangosuthu Buthelezi would re-enter the process of negotiations aimed at creating a democratic South Africa. You know, the good ol' chief feels more comfortable when he is inside than when he is languishing in the cold outside. That's why they call him *Umtwana wakwa Pindangene* (one who will always re-enter). Welcome aboard, Shenge.

Remember me, Madiba?

Ever wondered how our transition to democracy was so strikingly similar to the events that will lead up to Judgement Day as predicted by disciple Matthew in his book in the Holy Bible? For those times in our history (April 1994), Matthew's chapter 7:21–23 has been interpreted thus: 'It's not everyone who says to me "Madiba, Madiba" who will enter the new South Africa, but only he who does the will of the ANC.

'Many will say on April 27: "Dr Mandela, Dr Mandela, did we not toyi-toyi in your name, and in your name drove out puppets and chant revolutionary slogans?"

'Then I (Mandela) will tell them plainly: "I never knew you. Away from me, you opportunists." '

That's perhaps why we had such a blessed transition.

Going bananas in the new SA

After the dawn of the new South Africa, cabinet ministers in the now defunct homelands have inevitably found themselves without jobs. But in what was then known as Gazankulu, a former cabinet minister has found a novel way of keeping himself busy and staying out of trouble: he is trying his hand at farming. As a former Gazankulu Minister of Agriculture, it was not surprising to see Chief Jackson Nhlaneki trying to turn barren land in his poverty-stricken village outside Giyani into a highly productive agricultural land where he is trying to grow bananas. Some thought Nhlaneki had gone bananas. But if you think about it, the chief was a little nostalgic about the good old days of apartheid. After serving a banana republic that was Gazankulu for so long, it was only natural for him to start his own banana republic right in his own backyard. As they say, you can take a homeland leader out of a banana republic, but you cannot take a banana republic out of him.

Good luck, chief, but don't step on those banana peels.

Sliding into nothingness

As South Africa witnessed the changing of the guard in 1994, one of the big questions that was on many people's lips was: what does the future hold for people who were regarded as Pretoria's puppets during the apartheid era? Fortune tellers agreed on one thing: they would all slide into nothingness. Kgosi Lucas Mangope, who once arrogantly and vehemently vowed his now defunct Bophuthatswana homeland would never be incorporated into South Africa 'in a hundred years', has suddenly run out of friends. He has also discovered that donkeys, which have a special biblical significance to Christians all over the world, have never forgiven him for what he did to them at the prime of his career when he ordered that they be shot on sight. You don't shoot a donkey and get away with it. It therefore appears that

the chief will have to apologise and make friends with these asses if he wants to lead a meaningful and fruitful life. If he doesn't, he may discover that life is really an ass.

In the north, Nelson Ramodike, former chief minister of the disbanded Lebowa homeland, is all tears as he watches his derailed gravy train go up in a pall of smoke. If he is lucky, and depending on the mood of Northern Province premier Ngoako Ramathlodi, Ramodike may get his job back as a traffic officer. Who knows, he may end up as president of South Africa one day. Even his namesake president Nelson Mandela started out as a mine policeman.

Down in the Eastern Cape, Oupa Gqozo, former military leader of the now defunct Ciskei homeland, is rumoured to be seriously considering starting a furniture business, which will be in direct competition with Joshua Doore. The motto of his business? 'You have an *oupa* in the furniture business.'

Choosing between hooker and politician

It is always perceived that politicians are in love with politics simply because of their love for power and

money. But is it really worth it when a hooker, of all people, can earn far more than the most powerful politician in the land? A few years ago a Johannesburg escort girl told a Johannesburg' newspaper that she earned a whopping R23 000 a month for selling sexual favours to anyone who cared to jump into bed with her.

Her salary amounted to R276 000 a year – R74 000 more than what the then state president F W de Klerk used to earn. What's more, the booty was tax free. After such revelations, who really wants to be a politician?

An empty and hollow shell

Soon after selling its Plein Street, Johannesburg, building to the African National Congress a few years ago, Shell SA suddenly found itself smiling all the way to the bank. Reason? The company started receiving miles and miles of free advertising space as major newspapers in the country and overseas continued to refer to the building as Shell House. Then came what was later to be the embarrassingly dubbed 'Shell House massacre' in which at least eleven so-called Zulu royalists were shot dead in front of the building a few days before the 1994 democratic general elections. There were murmurs in the company's headquarters in Cape Town that it was time that the ANC changed the name of the building. That was, however, not to happen. Now that relative peace and tranquillity have returned to the country and the ANC finds itself in government, Shell's executives are not so sure whether to rejoice or to weep. Shell House is no longer in the news and neither is Shell. The building has become, save for a few pieces of furniture and a couple of people, an empty shell.

His Majesty who?

Controversial Chief Mangosuthu Buthelezi has given some newspapers a dressing down for 'undermining' King Goodwill Zwelithini by 'disrepectfully' addressing him by his first name. The good ol' chief probably has a point – no one should be on a first name basis with a person of the king's stature. But the chief probably does not know that in Nongoma, right in the king's backyard and heart of the Zulu kingdom, people address *iSilo samabandla*, His Majesty the honourable King of the Zulus simply as *ubut' Zweli* (brother Zweli or, if you like, *bra* Zweli).

Charity, bra, begins at home!

Masters of gobbledygook

Former Minister of Constitutional Development Chris Heunis's public utterances were, as you would expect from a Nat, not always politically correct. Described as a master of gobbledygook and malapropism, Heunis was a hardened journalist's nightmare because he was in the habit of saying things he did not mean. But if you loved Chris Heunis, you will almost certainly dig Mark Mfikoe, former president of the Azanian Students' Convention. Mfikoe once took issue with a Johannesburg newspaper for quoting him as having said: 'The political playing fields in Bophuthatswana have been levelled by Mangope's refusal to meet students' demands.'

He then sent a fax to set the record straight. His correct words, he said, were: 'To strive for free political activity in Bophuthatswana should be equated with the political tolerance of the repressive system that the Bophuthatswana regime is because in essence, as the parameters of political activism widen so diminishes the room for political repression because political repression and liberation cannot exist in one room.' Phew!

BC at work

The Azanian Youth Organisation apparently holds the view that if you can't beat them, join them. Realising that it was fighting a losing battle against township thieves, Azayo – the youth wing of the Black Consciousness Movement – has embarked on a campaign to speak to thugs in the language they understand: *tsotsi taal*.

The organisation is issuing bumper stickers that, it hopes, will lessen the incidence of car hijackings and thefts in the townships. The sticker reads: '*Asispini elokishini. Asikhawati udarkie.* (We don't "operate" in the township. We don't target a black).'

Is this what they mean by Black Consciousness?

Water in a Rocky mountain

Now that Rocky Malebane-Metsing has become a *persona non grata* in his own backyard, wouldn't it be better for him to move on and just get on with his life? I'm quite sure that Northern Province premier Ngoako Ramatlhodi, whose region has been devastated by drought for many years, will welcome Mr Malebane-Metsing with open arms, even though he would risk being censured by the organisation both men belong to – the African National Congress.

You see, the surname Metsing is derived from the word *metsi*, a Sotho-Tswana word for water. And water is exactly what Mr Ramatlhodi desperately needs at the moment.

One man's poison, you would say, is another man's water.

Who is going to catch this train?

The runaway gravy train has received unprecedented publicity since the government of national unity took over the reins of power from the Nats. Strangely enough, no one has spoken to, heard or seen the driver. After several months in the fast lane, we can finally unmask the identity of the driver. He is none other than Minister Trevor Manuel, who was once Minister of Trade and Industry – two of the most important money-spinning sectors in the South African economy.

Although the goods-laden train is moving at a breathtaking speed, the minister's colleagues in the Government feel Manuel is not moving fast enough as he has put the train only on *manuel*. The colleagues, most of whom are members of parliament who want an increase in their already fat pay packets, say Manuel must put the train on automatic for it to move a little bit faster. But to his colleagues' disappointment, Manuel seems to have lost the operating manual.

FOUR

Sport, Health and Fitness

When soccerites go for lunch

When it comes to matters horseracing, James 'Jimmy BoHorse' Maphiri is an authority. But I'm not sure if the same can be said about him when the subject is soccer. Some time ago Maphiri was assigned by Radio Metro, the action station 'in a class by itself', to cover the international friendly game between Mamelodi Sundowns and Sheffield Wednesday at Loftus Versfeld. As the players were trooping back onto the field for the second half, good ol' Maphiri told millions of listeners that the players were coming back from lunch.

Perhaps Bra Jimmy was telling us something we didn't know. Horses, we can safely deduce, go for lunch in between races.

Dropping his balls

In an apparent attempt to fill the gap created by a wage strike at the SABC a few years ago, a certain English radio station sent one of its DJs to do a commentary on the Castle Challenge Cup Final between Fairways Stars and Cape Town Spurs at FNB Stadium. The poor DJ had apparently not seen a soccer pitch before, let alone watched grown-up men kicking the pig-skin around.

The Fairways Stars goalkeeper repeatedly got a dressing down from the DJ, who kept on accusing him of 'dropping his balls' every time he tried to save the ball from sailing into the net. What a mouthful!

Going into the third half

Then there was this Radio Xhosa commentator who appeared to be more familiar with the oval-shaped rugby ball than the spherical-shaped football who was covering a Cup game between Moroka Swallows and, coincidentally, Cape Town Spurs at Athlone Stadium. When the game went into extra time, the commentator confidently told his listeners that the game was going into the third half. My maths teacher would kill me if ever I said that.

Chicken feed on the football field

So Roosters have chickened out as sponsors of National Soccer League's First Division club Mamelodi Sundowns. It had to happen. The Mamelodi ensemble had started to become chicken feed on the football field, so much so that the relationship between the two parties was no longer finger lickin' good. Besides, the then coach Jeff Butler had this penchant of getting it where the chicken got it – in the neck. To protect the controversial coach from ending up in the frying pan like most chickens do, the chicken franchise had to pull out. Now that Sundowns are being sponsored by a furniture company their biggest worry may be that they might end up as part of the furniture at Ellerines.

Peck
Peck

Balls, and more balls

The SABC seemingly also does not want to be left behind when it comes to baring it all. Urging sports enthusiasts to attend its international sports expo at the Kyalami Exhibition Centre in Johannesburg some time ago, SABC 2's sports programme *Topsport* placed an ad in Johannesburg newspapers saying, in part: 'If you want to see more than just balls, this one's for you.'

Names which degrade the nation

What should our national soccer squad really be called? Although 'Bafana Bafana' has somehow become sacrosanct, there are some people who continue to show uneasiness and discomfort with the nickname, given unilaterally by an unnamed soccer scribe. A Sunday newspaper entered the fray when it canvassed opinions from its readers. Most of them said they did not like the nickname Bafana Bafana because it 'degraded the nation'. Instead they came up with very interesting suggestions.

An Orlando East, Soweto, reader suggested that the squad be called the Burning Spears. Nice name, especially if you take into consideration the fact that we South Africans are obsessed with traditional weapons with which we try to eliminate one another. Besides, a squad with a name like that will always spell disaster for any opposition. The problem is that the players will most probably resort to violence every time they lose.

Then there was a suggestion from a Kagiso reader that the squad be called the Mighty Crocodiles. I also do not have any qualms about this one. But do I hear *Die Groot Krokodil* P W Botha saying from the Wilderness: 'You can't really forget me, can you?'

A fan from Pretoria suggested the name Mandela Stars. Good, as long as it is not confused with, or takes a leaf from, the notorious but now disbanded Mandela Football Club which was well known for taking on its 'opposition' outside the soccer field.

Another reader said Lions of the South would be a perfect name for our boys. Do I hear former ANC Youth League president Peter Mokaba chanting: 'Roar, young lions, roar!!!'? The main problem with this name is that the players will spend the entire 90 minutes toyi-toying instead of knocking the ball around.

Why Clive Barker is called a dog

What is in a name? A lot, especially if your name is Clive Barker, coach of the South African national soccer team who led the country to many important triumphs, including the 1996 African Cup of Nations, since taking over from Chilean-born manager Augusto Palacios. In fact, sources within the national squad say it's the mere mention of his name that propels our players to display almost magical performances. Every time he barks – yes, barks – instructions from the bench, the players start picturing in their minds a mean-looking dog ready to plunge its venomous fangs into the flesh of anyone who dares defy him. Some of my unreliable and lowly placed sources say Barker also goes by the name 'Dog'.

Now, why would anyone on earth call our beloved coach a dog when the least he deserves is a compliment for a job well done? Because, they say, a Barker is something that barks – which is a dog. This perhaps goes to show why our very first national coach, Stanley 'Screamer' Tshabalala, was not as successful. A bark, it now seems, is better than a scream.

The boot was on the other foot

One of the nicest things about being a sports journalist is
that you don't only rub shoulders with high-profile personalities in the mink and manure world but are always
pampered with presents by clubs, sponsors and sports
organisations. The presents are not meant to bribe journalists into writing favourably about certain organisations, as some people may hasten to think, but are a
token of appreciation aimed at further bolstering working relationships between the media, sports organisations and clubs. The presents can come in any form,
from bottles of whisky to baseball caps, from tracksuits
to T-shirts. So sports editors of various publications
must have thought the boot was on the other foot when
they received an invitation from the Soweto Olympic
Sports Congress to attend the launch of the British-SA
Initiative at Orlando Stadium in Soweto. The invitation
to the sports editors concluded by saying: 'Your presents
will be highly appreciated.' No wonder many sports
journalists stayed away from the function!

Mixing up the cards

Now that the Orlando Pirates-Kaizer Chiefs BobSave
Superbowl saga of a few years ago is finally over, the
truth can now be told. The violence that erupted at the
FNB Stadium when the two sides locked horns was
sparked off by a very rare incident. It is said that when
referee Ian McLeod cautioned Pirates' Marks
Maponyane, instead of showing the player a yellow

card, he inadvertently produced his (McLeod's) Kaizer Chiefs' membership card, which is also yellow in colour, and flashed it across the Pirates midfielder's face. The hawk-eyed Pirates supporters saw red and started pelting McLeod with an assortment of missiles. Now can you see why McLeod is justified in blaming the National Soccer League for failing to inform him in time that he was going to officiate in this game? He must have mixed up his Chiefs' membership card and yellow cards when he left for the airport in a hurry.

Flying on borrowed feathers

Have you ever seen or heard of birds which are scared of heights? Well, I have. They go by the name of Moroka Swallows Limited. After nestling at the top of the 1993 first division league log – where they should actually belong – the Dube Birds started losing their rhythm, as they usually do when a lot is expected of them. Is it, then, true that David Chabeli's Birds are always flying in borrowed feathers?

The rebelling Darkies

When the Nelspruit community came together some years ago to form a soccer club, they thought Dangerous Darkies would be a nice name for the new baby. When the club was promoted to the First Division of the National Soccer League, the baby started growing into a monster which became too hot to handle and too dangerous to manage. The players did all sorts of dangerous things, like rebelling against the owners and threatening not to honour fixtures. The owners heaved a big sigh of relief when one Fani Molapo bought the club for an undisclosed fee. After experiencing innumerable problems, Molapo then duly changed the name of the club to Ruto Callies.

Boxing and the black magic

The hiring of former newspaper editor Jack Blades as public relations officer for the Jacob 'Baby Jake' Matlala camp is, in more ways than one, the biggest scoop ever in local boxing history. There is no doubt that Blades, one of the most innovative and talented newspapermen I've ever known, will give his best shot in developing and sustaining Matlala's image. Mate, as Jack is popularly known among his peers and fellow journalists is, however, known for something else: his obsession with muti and his undivided belief in black magic. This dates back to the time when he started editing the Extra edition of the *Sunday Times*. So boxing fans can be excused for thinking, rightly or wrongly, that Blades is going to play a dual role in the diminutive fighter's boxing career – being a public relations officer by day and a mutiman by night. If, for example, he sprinkles muti in the ring the night before the fight and Baby Jake goes on to win it, we'll all be happy, I'm sure.

Ride on, mate.

Running away from fortunes

With boxer Dingaan Thobela's star on the wane, his trainer Norman Hlabane had, until recently, reason to look for greener pastures as he wasn't too sure if there would be food on the table for very long. A strict disciplinarian, Hlabane then remembered a young man in his camp who was at the ringside when Thobela fought Tony Lopez in Sacramento in the United States some time ago. The young man who, like Thobela, hails from Tshiawelo, Soweto, had fought a few fights and had made a good account of himself at home. Hlabane thought of giving him a chance as the boy had shown talent enough to be South Africa's future champion. He phoned him up and said he would pick him up so they would go to the gym and start serious training. The young man agreed. When the ecstatic Hlabane arrived at the young man's home, our prospective future champion wasn't there. Extremely disappointed, Hlabane got back into his car and drove to the gym on his own. He had hardly turned the corner when the young man emerged from the nearby bushes, visibly relieved. Perhaps it was high time in this country that we coined an adage like this: You can take a boxer to the ring but you cannot make him fight.

Black like Tony Lopez

Huge South African companies get a lot of mileage out of persuading well-known sports personalities to endorse their goods and services, in exchange for cash. It is a marketing strategy that has always worked wonders but the local hair care firm that was co-sponsoring the Dingaan Thobela-Tony Lopez grudge fight at Sun City in 1993 took it a little bit too far. A lot of people may have thought they were dreaming when they saw the Sacramento Tiger walking around The Lost City in a 'Black Like Me' T-shirt a few days before the fight. Now, if Lopez is black like you and me, who wants to be black?

Follow the drunken elephants

Do you know why Moroka Swallows are huffing and puffing on the field of play these days? The once high-flying Dube Birds have been immobilised and the blame has been put squarely on the shoulders of their new sponsors – Elephant Beer. Now the Birds no longer fly high. Instead they walk like drunken elephants. Perhaps it is also time that their slogan is changed to: 'Don't follow me, follow the drunken elephants.'

Unknown King Nobody

When Mamelodi Sundowns' Kenny Niemach sank top English premier division side Leeds United with a magnificent goal at Loftus Versfeld in the United Bank Challenge, he was hailed as a new soccer hero. And when the relatively unknown Ruud Gullit lookalike went on to humiliate Kaizer Chiefs by banging in two of his side's three goals in the final of the same competition a couple of days later, he was elevated to the status of a

king. So when he went to FNB Stadium to face the same Chiefs a week later, many people said he would bury the once glamour team under an avalanche of goals. But that was not to happen. Instead he was played off the park by diligent Chiefs' defenders who reduced him to a soccer nonentity. By the end of the game, he was no longer known as Kenny Niemach, but as Kenny Niemand, the Afrikaans word for 'nobody'.

It's quarter-past anytime

If you still don't believe there is such a thing as 'African time', go to Swaziland. It is one country where African time is observed so religiously that anyone who preaches punctuality is looked upon with disdain. The other day hundreds of soccer fans went to Somhlolo Stadium in Mbabane to watch two of the country's top teams in action. The kick-off was tentatively – yes, tentatively – scheduled for 3 pm but the game did not start until about one and a half hours later, something that did not bother the fans. As a result, the game was still on when the sun set. It was almost pitch dark when a member of the losing team decided, deliberately or otherwise, to kick the ball out of the unlit stadium into the nearby bushes. The players and official went out to look for the ball but it was nowhere to be found. A replay was then ordered to take place another time and another day. No one was bothered as to the exact time and date because, after all, there is no hurry in Swaziland.

Condoms that stand up to the test

When the Aids epidemic started spreading its dreaded tentacles across the globe, very few people realised it would bring with it conditions conducive to healthy, yes healthy, business practices. Like all businesses, condom manufacturers are these days faced with stiff competition, if you will excuse the pun, wherever they try to penetrate the market. There was, for instance, a certain Malaysia-based company that did some research before venturing into the unique South African market. Their research, thank goodness, turned out to be worth it. The company, to its surprise, discovered that the South African-made condom had to be a 'little bit longer than normal' – that is to say a little longer than they make them in Eastern countries.

Now another company, known only as Mates Healthcare SA, has thrust itself onto the scene. And by the look of things there is, if you like, a long and bruising battle ahead. Mates Healthcare SA does not only promise good quality condoms but it proudly claims its condoms can hold over two buckets of, wait for it, water. Not only that, the company claims its condoms can be stretched up to 152 centimetres. That's more than 1,5 metres, or five feet long for those not familiar with the metric system. With a condom as voluminous and as long as that, who could complain that he is not being catered for? People who doubt these claims can really stand up – pun not intended – will simply have to take it on good faith. Especially if they do not have equipment for extensive testing.

Can you read this prescription?

Ever wondered why our boys in blue seem not to be getting along well with our medical doctors? Well, it has something to do with the unique way the doctors dot their 'i's' and cross their 't's'. (If you didn't know, all our doctors went to the same handwriting school.) This has apparently led to many police investigating officers having difficulties in deciphering the doctors' reports – causing delays, misunderstandings and confusion in the process. To avoid this, doctors who are called upon to complete police reports to help with criminal investigations are now being asked to do so in a LEGIBLE handwriting. Isn't it time that we also ask the same for our prescriptions?

Learning about marital arts

Owners of a Johannesburg gym may succeed where social workers and agony columnists have failed. If a price list distributed around the Johannesburg area is anything to go by, Min's Gym at Nuworld Entertain-

ment Complex, formerly Shareworld, is a unique fitness centre in the world. The gym lists marital arts as one of the services it provides to its clients and would-be clients. I suspect that the gym not only takes you through the fitness paces, it also gives you tips on how to survive marital storms and be a good sex partner. Isn't this what we need in the new South Africa?

PS: I wonder if the gym offers martial arts as well?

Lead the way, kwacha

Five doctors have come together to form a holding company for black medical practitioners. The company, according to *Enterprise*, a fast-growing black monthly business magazine, is called Kwacha. The magazine says Kwacha, which has an issued capital of 300 000 shares of R1 each, is 'causing ripples in the health industry'. So far, so good. But as to what the name means, your guess is as good as mine.

One can only hope that the company does not follow in the footsteps of the Zambian currency, also known as kwacha, on the way to the doldrums.

FIVE

Education

Closing the doors of learning

With the new education dispensation firmly in place, one would think the days when black pupils and teachers would give themselves unofficial time off under the guise of class boycotts and stayaways would now be a thing of the past. Not so. At least not at Vuwani High School in Tshiawelo, Soweto. Pupils went to school one Monday morning as usual only to be told later to go back home. Reason? The keys to the classrooms, apparently kept in the principal's office, had been stolen during a break-in over the weekend. It is an open secret that the pupils, and some teachers I guess, received the announcement with open arms, especially since it was a Blue Monday.

Talk about opening the doors of learning.

Cheating teacher

It is not only pupils and students who dread exam time. A Northern Province teacher, who was a part-time student at the University of South Africa, found that the exams came too soon for him when he sat for his History paper. The teacher then started 'referring' – a politically correct term for cribbing – to some study

TEACHER

CHEATER

material hidden under his desk when the going got tough. The invigilator wasted no time in throwing the cheating teacher out of the exam room and disqualified him from the entire examination. If some of our teachers are cheats, who is going to teach our children?

Pay day, then toyi-toyi

Question: Why is it that teachers embark on protest action just after pay day and not in the middle of the month?

Answer: Because a teacher cannot toyi-toyi on an empty and dry stomach.

Who is going to teach the teachers?

Parents whose little kids spend most of their weekdays at a Soweto créche were shocked, and understandably so, to receive the following letter from the headmaster:

Dear parents/guardian

We are hereby inviting you to pay your child the following amount: R15 for graduation ceremony before 29/11/92. R20 for a trip to Shereworld per child and guardian before 14/11/92.

We would wish to appreceate your curperation.

Yours sincerely

The headmater

Aggrey who?

Sowetan Editor-In-Chief Aggrey Klaaste is probably the most popular and well-known black newspaperman in South Africa today. A well-travelled intellectual and a perfect role model, Klaaste has graced many a conference room throughout South Africa where his speeches on nation building have captivated audiences and moved many others to act positively and contribute towards rescuing South Africa from social ruin. Yet Klaaste is not known in his own backyard – Soweto. Asked who the Editor-In-Chief of *Sowetan* was at a Soweto beauty contest at Club Status, Fun Valley Pleasure Resort, just outside Soweto, a young beauty queen confidently looked at the judge and shouted at the top of her voice: 'Mbuzeni Zulu.' Mbuzeni Zulu, one of the newspaper's photographers, was there and was not amused.

However, children in the white suburbs can claim to be doing much better on this score. At a school function in the northern suburbs the other day, a young white kid, who must have seen Klaaste on TV on several occasions before, walked up to him and said: 'Good afternoon, Mr Agony Klaaste.'

A bird called mosquito

If there are still people who do not know who Aggrey Klaaste is, does it surprise you that there are those who do not know what an owl is? A contest in a TV quiz show stunned millions of viewers the other night. Asked what a bird which preyed at night was called, the contestant, to the embarrassment of the show hosts, bellowed the answer: 'Mosquito!'

Teaching the teachers

If you needed a graphic illustration of how bad apartheid education really was, you should have been at a teachers' demonstration in Eldorado Park, south of Johannesburg, the other day. The teachers were demonstrating against the Azanian Students' Movement's campaign to drive white teachers out of township schools.

One of the teachers was carrying a placard which read: '*Azikho Azapo*. Leave Our **Teacers** Alone.'

Now, if a teacher cannot spell a word like teacher, who is going to teach our children how to spell?

Caption writing is an ass

Abbreviations and acronyms always make our lives easier because we don't have to say Congress of Traditional Leaders of South Africa when we can say Contralesa. But this does not give us a licence to abbreviate any word that comes to mind, like someone did on

TV the other day – the caption writer called someone an Ass Director when all he needed to say was Assistant Director. It wouldn't sound nice, either, to say the Civics Ass of Southern Transvaal, would it?

Thanks for your clinicality

The Queen can no longer claim to be in control of the English language as its horizons are being constantly widened all over the world to suit particular circumstances, needs and tastes. Irrespective of what people may say, this transformation is good for the language as it becomes richer and richer in the process, with new phrases being coined and new words being created. At a party the other day a guest who had obviously enjoyed himself to the fullest wanted to demonstrate his appreciation to his host for an evening well spent. The guest walked up to his host and said: 'Thank you very much for your hospitality and clinicality.' This goes to show that if hospitals are seen as places of fun, so should be clinics.

Who is Ken Owen?

The *Sunday Times*, with a weekly readership of around 500 000, is undoubtedly the most widely read Sunday newspaper in the country. But I know someone who does not read it. He is Transvaal Judge President, C F Eloff, who tried and subsequently sentenced to death Janus Walusz and Clive Derby-Lewis for the murder of former South African Communist Party general secretary Chris Hani.

Judge Eloff must have shocked quite a few people during the trial proceedings in the Rand Supreme Court when he asked: 'Who is Ken Owen?'

Ken Owen, as you might or might not know, was at the time Editor of the *Sunday Times*. His name was also on the hit list found by police in Walusz's flat shortly after his arrest, a fact which was widely published in the press, including the *Sunday Times*. If one of our learned judges does not know who Ken Owen is, who would really want to kill Ken Owen? But then the learned judge is doing himself a disservice by shunning the newspaper. He is denying himself the pleasure of looking at the sexy back page pin-up girls, which had been the newspaper's trademark since time immemorial.

SIX

Sex, Fashion and Trends

Fashion: the naked truth

Who says you have to be all dressed up to stand a chance of scooping an award for being the world's best dressed person these days? If the criteria used by a Los Angeles based fashion watcher can be taken as a yardstick, people like our own and only Beau Brummel, who enjoy appearing in public in their birthday suits, now have a justifiable right to lay claim to this prestigious title. This leading American fashion watcher, whom we know only as Blackwell, surprised many people recently when he named top American actress Sharon Stone as one of the world's best dressed women, along with Princess Di and a few others. Many movie goers will vividly remember Stone in the box-office hit *Basic Instinct*, in which she plays the role of Catherine Tramell, a sexy and wealthy American author who is at the centre of a murder investigation. The part for which many people particularly remember her, more than anything, is the one in which she clearly shows she does not feel very comfortable walking around with her panties on. That's the part that Blackwell also probably remembers very well.

Not only that, Stone once took her clothes off and posed nude for *Playboy* magazine. So, how do you call someone who obviously hates clothes a best dressed person? Blackwell is probably trying to tell us the naked truth: for your sanity to be restored in this confused and confusing global village, go back to basics – the biblical era of Adam and Eve.

The taste that's come to Lite

The South African Breweries, after accepting that beer drinking is not only the preserve of men, has come up with a new beer that is expected to go down well, if you like, with women guzzlers. No sooner had Castle Lite started hitting the shebeens, taverns and pubs than questions about who concocted and brewed the nice tasting beer began filling the air. Someone has whispered in my ear that Castle Lite was brewed many moons ago by Charles Glass's better half. Her name, according to my unreliable and lowly placed sources, is Sheila Glass and she is black. People who have tasted Castle Lite say if ever there was a taste that had stood the test of time, this was it.

Perhaps the colour of Sheila Glass's skin explains why black women in South Africa outdrink the entire white beer market. Anyone out there want to join the Sheila Glass Society?

Taking the brrr! out of winter

You certainly have heard about garden parties and kitchen parties but you probably have not heard about pyjama parties. Well, these parties are gradually, so I'm told, becoming an in thing in Soweto and are even threatening to strip, if you could please excuse the pun, the *stswetsa* dance of its popularity title. As to what people do at these parties, your guess is as good as mine. But it seems these all-night parties have apparently been designed to take 'the brrr!' out of winter.

Sitting on a goldmine

The suggestion by the Western Cape region of the ANC some time ago to raise funds by auctioning some of President Nelson Mandela's personal possessions – such as shoes – to pay off its R264 000 post-election bill, could be a smart idea for the Reconstruction and Development Programme. Many of our politicians have valuable personal possessions with historical and cultural significance that could help boost the coffers of the RDP. Topping the list is obviously Mrs Winnie Mandela's designer hat which, if you remember, became a counter-attraction at the inauguration of her estranged husband as the first black president of South Africa at the Union Buildings in Pretoria on May 10, 1994. The hat, which hasn't stopped tongues from wagging ever since, could fetch hundreds of thousands of rands for the RDP at any auction anywhere in the world.

Then there is Chief Mangosuthu Buthelezi's ceremonial stick, which he carries everywhere, apparently even in his sleep. Dubbed 'The Mother of All Cultural

Weapons', the stick is one of the most important and invaluable possessions the country has ever had.

Another personal possession that could fetch a few thousand dollars at Sotheby's is the old and battered chauffeur driven Peugeot 404 that was used by the late Zephania Mothopeng, former president of the Pan Africanist Congress, before his death. This is the car that took the Lion of Azania to all the places his official duties required him to be, while his peers in the libera-

tion movement basked in state-of-the-art automobiles. Even though it had to be push-started at times, it always huffed and puffed its way to its destination, no matter how far.

Afrikaner Weerstandsbeweging leader Eugène Terre'Blanche may be a thorn in the flesh of most South Africans, but he is unwittingly sitting on a goldmine right now – his torn green underwear. Probably the most talked-about green underwear in the world, there is no doubt it has the potential to fetch up to R1 million at the auction. What an incentive this would be for the RDP.

Sexy Sexwale

He does not know it but Tokyo Sexwale, premier of the Gauteng region, is breaking up marriages. It all started when he became an instant TV star after the assassination in 1993 of his closest friend and South African Communist Party boss Chris Hani. Every time the likeable Sexwale appeared on the gogglebox, a certain woman would become excited and tell her husband, in the presence of other people, how sexy, handsome and intelligent the ANC man was. She was even overheard cursing her gods for not having made it possible for Sexwale and herself to be romantically linked before she made a lifetime commitment to her husband, which she was now regretting. My sympathies go to the poor hubby.

Most sought after heart-throbs

Have you ever wondered what housewives in the Johannesburg northern suburbs do when their husbands are away sweating it out in the concrete jungles of Gauteng? Left to take care of the household chores, the madams of the 'kitchens', as suburbs are sometimes known, must be bored to the bone by the monotonous lifestyle they lead. But they also get a chance of baring their souls, to whomever cares to listen, on the radio. When Radio 702 opened the lines and gave people an opportunity to choose high-profile figures they thought had charisma and sex appeal, the calls came in thick and fast. Guess who topped the list of charismatic heart-throbs who made women's hearts beat faster every time their names were mentioned either on TV or radio? Roelf Meyer, General Secretary of the National Party and Tokyo Sexwale, Premier of Gauteng!

In Sexwale's case, perhaps the first three letters of his surname have something to do with it. But the results of the station's survey will give those hard working, suffering gentlemen of the northern suburbs something to think about.

Life at seventysomething

Who says life begins at fortysomething?

He or she had better think again because life, as some people see it, actually begins at seventysomething. A seventy-two-year-old man once wrote a letter to the pen pal column of a Johannesburg newspaper and asked for correspondence from females who were 'prepared to settle down'. Are there any takers out there?

Dogs that lack the bite

Ever wondered why signs such as 'Beware of the Dog' in the townships have now been replaced by signs which read: 'Never mind the Dog, Beware of the Owner'? Researchers say dogs in South Africa's black townships can bark as much as they like; what they (the dogs) don't know is that they lack the bite. According to the researchers, not only do township dogs have a low life expectancy, their threat of causing injury from a

serious bite is extremely low. It appears from these findings that there will soon come a time when pet owners
will live in kennels to protect their dogs – which would
be living in comfort in their owners' houses – against
intruders and thieves. If I were an animal lover, I would
in the light of this give my dog a bad name and hang
him.

The Black Man's Wish

For many people, their ultimate wish in life is to find
themselves behind the steering wheel of a top of the
range BMW. Driving a Three Series 'Dolphin', as the
latest model of the luxury German-made car is popularly known in the townships, is not only a status sym-
bol but a show of power and wealth. But to many blacks
driving a BMW, let alone owning it, will remain just that
– a wish. They know they will have to fork out about
R120 000 for (by the standards of luxury cars) an ordinary middle of the road BMW model. While we all know
that BMW stands for Bayerische Motoren Werke, to
many blacks the abbreviation can only stand for: Black
Man's Wish.

Stoned under the table

Columnist Barry Ronge is undoubtedly one of the best
film critics and entertainment writers the country has
ever produced. He has, during his illustrious career
spanning several years, interviewed many of the heavy-
weights in the lucrative and glamorous industry world-

wide who, to many of us, seem immortal and untouchable. So it wasn't quite a surprise when Ronge found himself at Cannes Film Festival having breakfast with Sharon Stone, the gorgeous American actress who made her name in *Basic Instinct*. Stone, or rather her *Basic Instinct* character Catherine Tramell, is a lady who is in the habit of crossing and uncrossing her legs at the most inopportune moments, especially if surrounded by men. So Ronge could be excused if he kept on looking under the breakfast table every time Stone said something suggestive.

Tutu, man with a good taste for cloth(es)

Desmond Tutu must have been wondering what the fuss was all about when he had a ton of bricks dropped on his head for daring to criticise President Nelson Mandela's casual dress and the shirts that hang over his trousers. The then Archbishop of Cape Town, you see, felt he had to criticise the president because he (Tutu) was an authority on fashion. As a man of the cloth, it seems, he knows more about the cloth than anybody else. Even designers such as Versace and Miyake do not come close. And when he talks about dress, he really means dress. That's perhaps why we always saw him wearing purple dresses wherever he went.

Made of sterner stuff

The Mates Healthcare SA, a highly successful condom manufacturer in South Africa, could not have appointed

a better person to the position of managing director. The soaring sales of condoms – from R7 million in 1987 to R25 million in 1995 – is an indication that Mr Ian Stern is sternly committed to curbing the spread of Aids in this country, a scourge that is threatening to wipe mankind off the face of the earth. At a time when there are serious doubts about the quality and resistance capabilities of some types of condom, Stern has assured the public that his products, including Rough Rider and Bareback, have a longer lifespan and – if you will excuse the pun – are made of sterner stuff. Every time he says this, one can almost feel the sternness in his voice.

Which Cola is the real McCoy?

The heated and bruising Cola war between two of South Africa's major soft drink companies has assumed extravagant proportions as they continue to wrestle for support in the marketplace. The first salvo was fired by the Amalgamated Beverages Industries when they claimed, among other things, that their product, Coca-Cola, was the *makoya* cola, meaning, in *tsotsi taal*, that Coke was the real McCoy in the soft drink industry. New Age Beverages, makers of Pepsi-Cola in South Africa, hit back. They found an opening when, as part of their social responsibility programme, they linked up with the South African National Council of Alcohol and Drug Abuse to create awareness of the dangers of drug addiction.

'If you're hooked,' their advertising billboards pro-claimed, 'here's a lifeline . . .'

Now, the billboards may very well have been saying: 'If you're hooked on Coke, here's a lifeline ... Pepsi-Cola.'

Obesity is lekker

Physically disadvantaged people, to use a 'politically correct' term, are a lucky lot. When Baragwanath Hospital issued a directive a few years ago warning nurses carrying 'excess weight' to shed it or else, many

people came to their defence and the directive was subsequently withdrawn. Now some fellas think that obesity is *lekker*. They contend that fat people, to use a 'politically incorrect' term, are a romantic, loving, sexy and caring lot. A man who describes himself as a 'well-mannered gentleman', wrote to a pen pal column of a Johannesburg newspaper and put himself on the market. He was specific about his choice of ladies: 'They should be aged between 22 and 26 and be of medium build (70 kg–90 kg).'

Remember the American singing duo called Two Tons of Fun?

SEVEN

Life and Death

Keeping coffers and coffins brimful

Undertakers in South Africa are now adopting aggress-
ive marketing strategies as competition becomes, if you
can excuse the pun, stiffer and stiffer. It's now just a matter of time before some of them enter the lucrative world
of soccer where club officials are always ready and will-
ing to have their clubs' names desecrated, so to speak, as
long as their coffers – as opposed to coffins – are kept
brimful. It won't be surprising to wake up one day and
find our soccer clubs campaigning under the auspices of
the new look Gauteng Crematorium Soccer League.
Such a league would obviously boost clubs with names
like Orlando General Undertakers Football Club whose
motto would, quite naturally, be: 'We'll bury them
alive.'

Opponents would include teams such as Majavajava
Funeral Parlour Giant Killers and Taung Coffin Makers
who, you guessed it, would always put the final nail in
the coffin. With such a league, soccer would be a very
exciting sport as it would be a matter of life and death,
compared to the big yawn it is today.

Career at a dead end?

Like all intelligent sportsmen, it was quite natural for one of our boxing heroes, Dingaan Thobela, to start some kind of a business while he still could. When Thobela opened a hair salon during the peak of his career a few years ago, there was nothing hair-raising about it, except that some people feared – without foundation, of course – that fame could go to his head. Then, after his career took a nosedive following two successive defeats at the hands of Orzubek Nazarov, Thobela decided to spread his business wings. In what could be described as a hair-raising venture, he and a friend opened a funeral parlour in the West Rand township of Mohlakeng, which later moved to Johannesburg. Does this mean that our former World Boxing Association lightweight champion's career is coming to a dead end now that he is dabbling with the dead?

Stiffy and deadly competition

Competition in the funeral undertaking business is not only becoming stiffer and stiffer these days – it has developed into a cut-throat affair in which only the fit can survive. This was clearly demonstrated when a Gauteng family, which earns a living, if you like, by burying the dearly departed, claimed a rival undertaker was bent on killing their flourishing business and burying it for good. The family went on to allege in a TV interview that their rival used deadly underground tactics, so to speak, to bring them down. According to the family, the culprit hired thugs who broke into their

97

funeral parlour in the dead of the night, stripped parts off their hearses and stole expensive coffin-lowering machines. Although the family sees this as a grave problem, they are confident that their unnamed rival does not stand a ghost of a chance in the business and are prepared to fight to the death for their right to trade. They are, however, prepared to bury the hatchet as long as their rival comes out into the open and starts practising established and transparent business methods.

Whichever way you look at it, it is evident that someone in this dangerous and deadly game has either got to adapt, or die.

Shortest route to heaven

The National Road Safety Council has for many years been concerned about the carnage taking place on South Africa's roads. The council has launched campaign after campaign educating us on how to stay alive. Not anymore. Instead the council is these days showing us the quickest and shortest route to heaven. How else does one explain its recent advertising campaign which encourages people who indulge in alcohol to 'take a taxi home ...'?

This is like leading the proverbial lamb to the slaughter because minibus taxis are now notoriously known, rightly or wrongly, as mobile coffins. In fact, the council should change the phrase to read: 'If you want to go to heaven, take a taxi home or ask a friend to take you there safely.'

Board this taxi and go to Jesus

Instead of being seen as a viable mode of transport, minibus taxis have become one of the biggest scourges in our country. They have been described as mobile coffins because of their owners' involvement in taxi wars that always seem to claim innocent lives. The taxi owners' contribution to the carnage on our roads also speaks volumes for the industry's image as far as the public is concerned. A Soweto taxi recently seemed to strengthen the view that minibus taxis are meant to take passengers to their final resting place when it was seen displaying a bumper sticker reading: 'Come to Jesus.'

Where is home?

Many Soweto taxis continue to display bumper stickers which read: 'Surely, the Soweto Taxi Association will take you home safely.'

Really?

Gravely correct

Political correctness in South Africa is firmly taking root in all spheres of life. But in the North West people are taking political correctness a little bit too deep – right into the grave. While many people would think that the politically correct name for the dead would be 'the dearly departed', in the North West they feel it is too heavy and inappropriate a term. Instead they prefer to call their dead 'our late population'.

Making a kill in this business

Who says funeral undertakers don't have a sense of humour? As funerals become one of the biggest money-spinning business ventures in this country, undertakers are using imaginative advertising and promotional campaigns to survive, if you may pardon the pun. One undertaker, who was losing business to a newly established funeral parlour, ran a campaign which promised clients: 'We look after the whole family.'

When people began flocking to the new business, another undertaker came up with the slogan: 'We look after you, from birth until death.' Not to be outclassed, a third came up with a real scorcher: 'We really look after you, from erection to resurrection.'

No prizes for guessing who of the three undertakers made the final kill, if you can excuse the pun again.

Humour that'll really slay you

Newspaper reporters all over the world are constantly on a collision course with sub-editors. After working as a sub-editor for a couple of years, I should know. Many reporters have a great sense of humour and regard sub-editors as foes who always want to suppress their God-given talent of 'telling it like it shouldn't be'. What is striking about the reporters' sense of humour is that it always seems to touch on death, a subject that is, you will agree, not funny at all. Take for example, this masterpiece: 'The *funeral* of the baby who died when the caravan in which she was sleeping was allegedly gutted by fire in Eden Park is to be buried in the Eastern Cape on Saturday.' Burying funerals, you will agree with me, is really something out of this world.

Then there is this classic caption: 'A crowd gathers around a *corpse* of a *dead* infant boy.' Maybe I'm too obtuse but I still have to come across 'the corpse of a *living* infant boy'.

Another creative piece of work that did not, fortunately or unfortunately, make it into columns of a certain newspaper, thanks to an alert sub, was: 'We carried in our sports pages the *death* of Bethuel Morolo.' I'm sure many people will stop buying a newspaper that starts to carry deaths on its pages.

And here is another blockbuster: 'The *body* of a sixty-seven-year-old man from Leokaneng village near Pietersburg was *found dead* in front of his house after he was apparently beaten *to death* on Saturday morning.' This man, I tell you, is so exceptional that he died twice.

With our boxes of stones, we'll ...

Who says stone-throwing is a destructive form of protest which must be discouraged at all costs? A photographer working for a Johannesburg-based morning newspaper would definitely wish to differ with this view. The newspaperman used the stone-throwing skills he learnt as a schoolboy growing up in the streets of Soweto to his advantage when two car thieves hijacked his car the other day. After he was tossed out of his vehicle, the photographer hitched a lift and begged the driver to stay on the tail of the thieves, who were already on their way to a 'chop shop' somewhere in the townships. As fate would have it, the thieves, who were unaware that they were being followed, stopped at a traffic light. In a flash, the newsman got out of the other car, picked up a huge stone nearby and hurled it through the window of his car with all his might. The thieves might have thought they were being shot at because they got out of the car like lightning and ran away as fast as their legs could carry them.

Now, that's what we call survival of the fittest.

Boris Yeltsin's closely guarded secret

Russian president Boris Yeltsin has seemingly provided an answer for couples who are dying to have baby girls, or those who want bouncing baby boys. In a TV interview, Yeltsin said that during his younger days he and his wife were so poor that they did not even have a bed or a table in their tiny room.

'We did everything on the floor. We even made love on the floor. That's perhaps why we have girls,' Yeltsin said.

There you have it. If you want a baby girl, make love on the floor. If you want a boy, go somewhere else.

The stalking Stals

Computers are probably the best thing to have ever happened to mankind. They can do almost anything under the sun – from correctly predicting the weather to flying an aeroplane. They can even work twenty-four hours a day without complaining or asking to go to the loo at regular intervals to have a smoke. My personal computer is no different. It can differentiate between good and bad, day and night, young and old, weak and strong. The other day I asked it to do some detective work on Dr Chris Stals, governor of the Reserve Bank, who must by now be in many people's little black books. Within a split second, it came back with a reply that it does not recognise the word Stals. The spell check function, which has done great detective work for me in the past, told me the person I was probably looking for either 'stalks' people or 'steals' from them, or both. Well! I know the good ol' doc wouldn't agree with this finding, let alone like it. But reducing one's take home salary, as an increase in the bank rate always does, should effectively be called legalised stealing. We saw Dr Stals stalking us for a long time, didn't we?

EIGHT

South Africa's 12th Official Lingo

Hola, ithini ringers MaGents?
(Hi! there, guys, what's new?)

After *splashing* himself to his satisfaction, Zakes put on his best *Jewish*, including his brand new and well-polished Lacoste *batu* – the latest on the market – and started preparing for his visit to *Sun City* where his younger brother had been spending time with *AmaGents* for the past few weeks.

Zakes will never forget *daai dag* when Kurrah, who had been *gefahlaka* by *stapiyas* for *repossessing* a *Chris Hani* from a washing line in the *kitchens* a few weeks earlier, was sent to the *university*. This was after his *majiane* had refused to represent him in *hof* at the last minute, insisting to be paid the *nyuku* in advance – four *clipper* to be precise.

Zakes tried to convince the *majiane*, Bra Tim Moroka, that he would *pandha* or *tabalaza* the *zag* the same day as he earned his living by *spinning* from *ngamulas* in town or, when things are bad, by holding *oxen* on the packed Soweto *gados*.

But Bra Tim stood by his guns. Zakes never forgave him and the poor lawyer is now Zakes' *Ghost* No 1.

As he left the matchbox house he shared with his *old timer* and his *magrizana*, Zakes felt a strong pang of thirst

106

hit his throat. He immediately decided to via his *sharp posie* around the corner where he hoped to crack some *cook*, possibly a *cellular*, from Aunt Lizzy and probably even borrow a *De Klerk* or two for the cab.

As he approached the spot, Zakes saw one of his *ghosts*, known as T-man, an *Oros van 'n ou*, sitting on the verandah and having a *spinza* with a *16V*, a gorgeous *sweet sixteen* never seen in this part of the world before.

This is the mismatch of the century, Zakes thought to himself. His mind immediately went to work and decided there and then to hit poor T-man with a *Corobrik*. If T-man were to *jump*, thought Zakes, he would *coward* him. He did not care if T-man ended in *hosie* and he at *Sun City*.

When he got to where the two people were sitting, Zakes gave his old *ghost* a *current*, offered his *ringers* to the *16V* and asked her why on earth was she wasting her time with a *barree* like T-man.

Somehow T-man got a *June-July* and fled the *lonjana*. Seeing that the *sweet sixteen* was beginning to *ngcwala*, Zakes did not waste time and went straight to Aunt Lizzy and asked her to prepare a *gauge*, even if it was a *spy kos*, for the *16V*. After Aunt Lizzy had said it was *moja*, he then started negotiating for a *stadium*, just in case he were to *skep* the gorgeous little girl.

It was while he was trying to convince her when three redhot *transis* – a *slahla matende*, a *skop* and a *Zola Budd* – screeched to a dusty halt outside the *sharp posie*.

By the time T-man and his gangsters, well-known spinners, got out of their *transis* with guns blazing,

Zakes knew the situation was terribly *ntswembu*. He was suddenly nowhere to be seen. There was no doubt that he had hit a *spoon down*.

If you have read all this *marakalas* up to this point and understood each and every word every step of the way, then you are either absolutely nuts, very intelligent or agree with millions of South Africans that this should have been made, and rightly so, the 12th official language of South Africa.

If, on the other hand, you didn't understand even this exciting drama-filled story, then you have no business to be living in the new South Africa. This is a fledgeling language which is spoken by millions of people across the length and breadth of our urban areas. But it is not the *tsotsi taal* they spoke during those days in Sophiatown. It is not a *vlaai taal* and neither is it fanagalo. It is the new generation lingo which has succeeded where English – the so-called international language – has failed: cutting across the cultural and social divide in our country, uniting the literate and the illiterate, the poor and the well-to-do, the educated and the uneducated, the old and the young.

It is a language, you would say, of people on the ground. It is a lingua franca which moves with the times and one which is influenced by current events, new developments and the latest in fashion. As times roll, so does its vocabulary become enriched with new words and fresh phrases. You don't have to go to school to master the language. You don't have to look up words or phrases in the dictionary or thesaurus to understand what they mean because most of them are self-explanatory.

Take, for instance, a 'Chris Hani'. This means a multi-coloured tracksuit made from a parachute-like material. It is the tracksuit that the former South African Communist Party general secretary was wearing on that fateful Saturday morning when he was mowed down in cold blood in his Dawn Park, Boksburg, home by Polish national Janusz Waluz.

Another phrase which is self-explanatory is 'in my time'. This means an elderly person. It is derived from the fact that most elderly people, especially those who grew up in Sophiatown, always preface their conversations with: 'In my time ...' The phrase is also derived from American singer Teddy Pendergrass's hit of the same title which he released after an automobile accident ended his hectic love life when he was paralysed from the waist down.

A synonym for the phrase is the word dinosaur, made famous in Stephen Spielberg's movie, *Jurassic Park*. Women who are on the wrong side of fifty but still possess their striking, natural and youthful beauty are called – wait for it, 'timeless classics'.

As this is a language which is based also on fears and mistrust, every lawyer is perceived to be a *majiane* – a professional liar who lies his way to success or triumph. This is very interesting because many of our politicians are lawyers by training – right from President Nelson Mandela down to premiers such as Mathews Phosa and

Ngoako Ramatlhodi. We know many politicians do not know the meaning of truth, but can they live with being called *bomajiane*? Whether people like it or not, this language is going to survive all storms. In fact, it is going to grow in leaps and bounds as we approach the 21st century.

Glossary (for your own survival)

Splash: to bathe or wash
Jewish: clothes
Batu: shoes
Bra: short for brother; also means close friend, irrespective of gender. Not to be confused with bra as in woman's bra.
Sun City: Diepkloof Prison
AmaGents: the guys; sometimes means thugs
Gefahlaka: arrested
Stapiya: police officer
Daai dag: that day
Repossess: steal
Chris Hani: a multi-coloured tracksuit made from parachute-like material
Kitchens: historically white suburbs
University: prison
Majiane: (liar) lawyer
Hof: court
Nyuku: money; also known as zag
Clipper: R100
Phanda/Tabalaza/Spin: raise money by crooked and criminal means
Zag: money, also known as *nyuku*
Ngamula: white person (direct translation means rich person)
Oxen: mugging
Gado: train
Ghost: enemy
Old timer: father

112

Magrizana: granny
Via: go
Sharp posie: shebeen for a selected few; also known as spot or *lonjana*
Crack: borrow
Cook: booze; also known as *spinza*
Cellular: a nip of brandy or whisky
De Klerk: R2 coin introduced in early 90s, coinciding with reform measures initiated by then State President F W de Klerk
Oros: a fat person
16V/sweet sixteen: good-looking teenage girl
Corobrik: taking someone's lover by violent or intimidating means
Jump: resist violently
Coward: beat up or injure
Hosie: hospital
Current: cold shoulder
Ringers: chatting
Barree: backward person; also known as a *moegoe*
June–July: getting the shivers
Gcwala: becoming interested
Gauge: food
Spy kos: junk food
Moja: OK
Stadium: place of sexual activity
Skep: elope or stay overnight with a woman
Transi: motor vehicle, derived from the word transport
Slahla matende: a cabriolet
Skop: Chevair, Commodore or Rekord vehicles

Zola Budd: Toyota Hi-Ace
Ntswembu: bad
Hit a spoon down: escaped
Marakalas: mish-mash

Tsotsi taal alive and well
by Don Mattera, poet, writer and journalist:

Cultural imperialism is a most damaging form of psychological repression, to a degree that those who are subjugated often become active participants in the successful implementation and perpetuation of the 'spirit, character and authority' of the imperialists. Language is the first to be assailed because of its power as a strong transmitter and articulator of resistance and opposition, and of religion, culture and art. The very essence and ethos of a people is intrinsically locked in its language. And when indigenous languages face destruction then a lingua franca or township patois emerges to communicate, sustain, protect and perpetuate all that is sacred in the collective human experience of such a people. It was no different in most of the sprawling and cosmopolitan areas of South Africa. Language, the art of *wietie*, *skollietaal* and *tsotsi taal* become shields of survival and weapons of attack. Often the street vocabulary was so densely encoded and colloquialised that some township inhabitants, *moegoes* or *barrees*, could not even keep pace with the innovative but rapidly changing lingo.

'*Ah wietie es ah wietie*,' Sophiatown's *ousies* and *die motaras* and *majietas* might declare when they wish to emphasise their acceptance of a verbal agreement, especially one of a sexual nature or even when they want to seal a pact or an oath of some kind. *Wietie, howl, cable, shoot my, sny my die ses stekkies* are synonymous words and expressions often directed at friends and which usually allude to requests that a joke or secret be divulged, or that an incident out of the ordinary be related with all the attendant gesticulation and preening. The art of *wietie*, the ability to tell tall tales, *kakpraat*, as it is sometimes dubbed, uniquely characterised the *umhlobomdala* (veteran) fraternity of the legendary Kofifi-Sophiatown era. The oppressed created their lingo and lifestyles in the vibrant streets of Alexandra Township, Fietas, Western and Eastern Native Townships – Die Kaas and George Goch. They were colourful human tapestries of laughter and tears, music and danger, poverty and plenty. Often stirring from their slumber like zombies. Day in, day out; shedding blood and dreams. Music, magic and madness.

Birth in, death out ...

But Sophiatown was not the only place where *wietie* was created. *Taal* innovators from Newclare (Madglera) and particularly Die Kaas, also widely contributed to and influenced the texture of the Kofifi patois. New and exciting phrases were coined and popularised which gave Sophiatown a sort of cult status coupled with a strange, mythical austerity above other multi-ethnic townships. Of course, some psychologists may argue that the bohemian tapestry of pomp and pageantry; the sharp wit, humour and satire often served as forms of escapism from the harsh socio-political realities of the day, veritable anaesthetics against the pain of heartbreak and personal failure which the people hid under thick layers of booze and revelry.

There was always a word or phrase for anything or anyone: *'Daai momeesch es aah bogree' 'aah imitasi'*, *'aah gosh'* or *'goshfine'* for a conman or pretender. And when someone had been arrested: *'Hy short'*, *'hy angle'* and *'hy's getiemie'*.

'Mission grand', *'es annakant dolly'*, *'symbollie'*, *'es tot-ataa'*, *'bayzin boogie'*, *'sweet job no smoke, no mkatakata'*all allude to being OK, just fine, thank you. *'Knoppe'* means things are bad.

'Hulle'tom ga-knoffel' or *'ga-brostol'*, *'ga-diendil'*, *'garee-iron'* or *'ga-wachisa'* all allude to being assaulted. Then there is *airvees, dogsmeat, die kecheens* or *die backroom* which are the names given to the servants' rooms in the former white areas where the 'boy' or the 'girl' slept and scraps of leftover food were taken for the boyfriend.

'Ek sê outie, wat short?' (What's wrong brother?)

'Shandees my reekate. Ek es nou-net ga-eltee van my ramp – aah nuwe hlongo. Vier magumtsha honde met lang gonies en aah donkielat het my koeigavang.' (I've have just been robbed by four dogs of my new watch. They had long knives and a baton.)

And so, the art of *wietie; die taal van die main ouens; die lingo van toeka, van Kofifi, Die Kaas en Madglera* has sur-vived Malan, Strijdom, Verwoerd, Vorster, P W Botha just like the people who were violently removed and robbed of their birthright have survived and triumphed

116

in part. And when the last sunset comes for the likes of me, others may follow the legacy of *die taal* in a form, texture and transliteration of their own. Some will definitely speak Kofifi while others may choose otherwise. But at least this time around it won't be a matter of survival purposes. It will be a matter of choice. No cultural imperialism, no coercion and no Stalinism. Just *wietie*. Just *isicamtho, just bua my ma se kind*.

NINE

Life As It Should Or Shouldn't Be

The Bisho Bloodbath

Vladimir: Hi there, Ron, old boy! I understand there was quite a scene at Besho, Shibo whatever the name is, last Monday?

Ron: The name is Bisho but I'm not quite sure about my pronunciation. Yes, it was quite a scene. This madman set his dogs on us and they started firing at us like a swarm of bees. People fell like flies. It was like a war.

Vladimir: Is it true that you were in the forefront of the march?

Ron: You know me, Vlad. I saw a hole in the stadium and said to myself: 'This is my chance.' I and a section of the crowd decided to run through it. But as you know, we never succeeded in what we were trying to achieve as we were stopped dead in our tracks by a hail of bullets.

Vladimir: You can't change, you know, Ron. You're the same old Ron I know. You're a Red through and through. Now, why did you run through a hole, what's so special about holes?

Ron: You know, we South Africans have a strange obsession with holes. You must know about the Jani Allan keyhole story by now, don't you?

Vladimir: Yes, I know. How many people were killed in this incident?

Ron: Twenty-eight.

Vladimir: My foot! That's quite a lot. You must be regretting this. How did you survive?

Ron: How did I survive? You know they don't call me the Scarlet Pimpernel for nothing. As for regretting the incident, I certainly don't have any regrets at all. It was a risk worth taking. You know as well as I do that there's no struggle without casualties. Besides, it never crossed my mind that these dogs would just open fire like that. Not with you, I mean, the whole world watching. They did and all hell broke loose. But I lay the blame for this massacre squarely on the shoulders of the South African government and its despot.

Vladimir: By the way, what's the name of this guy you call despot?

Ron: They call him Oupa. It's Afrikaans for grandpa. You can call him a 'grandpa in the massacre business', if you like.

Vladimir: Tell me, Ron, what would you have done if these soldiers hadn't stopped you dead in your tracks?

Ron: Our mission was to occupy Bisho. We wanted to create a crisis for this guy Gqozo until he resigned.

Vladimir: What steps were you going to take after his resignation then?

Ron: You know, we hadn't quite given that much thought. But, as they say, we were going to cross that river when we reached it. Look, Vlad, I've got to run. I'll give you a call soon. It was nice talking to you on the phone since I last saw you in exile.

Vladimir: Good luck. Bye.

Who got what for Christmas '92 and why

Thank God, it's Christmas again. It's that time of the year when gifts, however small or modest, change hands in a spirit of goodwill. I would like to, in the same spirit, hand over a few Christmas goodies to a selected few for the contributions they made to the new South Africa. If your name is not on the list, please don't despair because your chance will come. Topping the short list of this year's recipients is none other than Afrikaner

Weerstandsbeweging (AWB) leader Eugène Terre'-Blanche. He will receive a six-legged man-size mobile toy horse in the next few weeks which he will ride whenever he and his band of khaki-clad neo-Nazi hooligans decide to stage a march on Shell House. He needs it, especially if you recall the unfortunate incident in Pretoria some time ago when he fell off his ageing horse after one of its legs had given in to his huge, sweaty frame.

While still on horses, I'm not forgetting my favourite racing commentator, James 'Jimmy BoHorse' Maphiri. How can I? A Tupperware lunch box, in which he will prepare lunch for my favourite horse, Thandabantu, is already in the mail. You see, Thandabantu goes for lunch after each and every race at the Market.

The Chief Minister of Lebowa, Mr Nelson Ramodike, will be the proud owner of a top-of-the-range, brand new Acitizeno watch come Christmas Day. The beauty of this South African-made watch, the good ol' chief minister and his civil servants will be happy to know, is that it is two hours faster than conventional watches, especially after lunchtime. With watches like that, they won't be caught napping when the clock hits the 2.30 pm *shayile* time.

In case you thought I was going to exclude controversial songbird Brenda Fassie, you're wrong because I'm going to send her Madonna's controversial book, *Sex*. What else can one give someone who says she is a Mafia in bed?

I did not know what to give ANC president Nelson Mandela for Christmas until Stalinist Harry Gwala gave me an idea the other day. I think a double-storey tin shack at Mandela View of his choice – there are so many of them scattered throughout the country – will do. At least Gwala would be reassured that Mandela had not betrayed the struggle when he moved to a posh house in one of the plush Johannesburg northern suburbs.

What could be the perfect Christmas present for Inkatha Freedom Party president Chief Mangosuthu Buthelezi than a copy of the book *Zulu Language Made Easy*. I assure him that the next time he calls a meeting of all IFP supporters at George Goch Hostel, he'll feel very comfortable when he addresses them in Zulu.

Kgosi Lucas Mangope, life president of the now defunct Bophuthatswana homeland, who has steadfastly resisted to have his tinpot incorporated into South Africa, will soon receive a leather-bound South African identity document, the first of its kind in the world, as a goodwill gesture. We can also have it gold-plated if he wants us to.

How can I forget Felicia 'While-I-was-still-in-America' Mabuza-Suttle? For her we have invented a special space shuttle which can only fly one way – downwards. This is the only space shuttle in the world which can help our adorable, high-flying Felicia find where Mother Earth is.

The South African Democratic Teachers' Union is one of my favourite trade unions in the country today, so there was no way in which it was not going to make the shortlist of individuals and organisations I intend to honour for their outstanding contributions during this turbulent year. After walking through the valley of the shadow of death which ended in the gnashing of teeth, what could be a more appropriate Christmas gift for Sadtu than a good shepherd who will have vision and leadership qualities to steer the union out of the confused political mess in which it finds itself ?

Turning to the airwaves again, *Agenda* presenter John Bishop really looks like he is out of this world with his extraordinary moustache. Seeing that it has seen better days, would it be a bad idea if he and Afrikaner Weerstandsbeweging leader Eugène Terre'Blanche were to swop their moustaches, even if only for a year or so? Perhaps it would make the programme a little livelier, don't you think?

Now for achievement awards: The Daydreamer of the Year Award goes to Brigadier Oupa Gqozo who at some stage woke up thinking he was a king.

The Chatterbox of the Year Award has been presented to musician Ray Chikapa Phiri, who once said: 'People don't talk, let's talk.' After his debut solo album of the same title proved a collossal flop, Phiri went into musical seclusion.

Your silence is deafening, Ray.

South Africa's most transparent meeting

At the start of the election campaign in February 1993 African National Congress leader Nelson Mandela and former State President P W Botha met for two and a half hours at *Die Groot Krokodil*'s Wilderness retirement residence. No newspaper or TV station reported on the talks, which took place at Mandela's request. The meeting took place at a time when South Africa was moving briskly into the new South Africa. My little fly on the wall managed, however, to eavesdrop and, in the interest of the public's right to know, brings you this edited version of the deliberations behind those closed doors:

Nelson Mandela: Good afternoon, Pieter. I was in the area trying to get a few votes for the ANC and I thought I should pay you a courtesy visit.

P W Botha: How good of you, Nelson. It's nice to know that there are people who care, especially when the chips are down and when one is in the twilight of one's life. Now, what can I really do for you?

Mandela: There's something that has been bothering me for a long time. We at the organisation thought you, as an objective Afrikaner with no political ambition at all, could help us in unravelling this mystery: where exactly can one find a *volkstaat*?

Botha: Haa! Haa! Haa! Do you also believe in that? There's no such a thing as a *volkstaat*. It's just a figment of someone's imagination. But let me warn you: be careful about this matter because it's a very emotive issue. There are louts who still believe there's a place in South Africa called a *volkstaat* even though it does not exist. It's *kêrels* like these who will lay down their lives for something like this. So be careful.

Mandela: Thank you very much for your advice. So, how has life been at the Wilderness?

Botha: To be honest with you, I feel like I'm really in the wilderness. There's no life here. I wake up in the morning and tend my garden. That's all. In the evening I try to work on my memoirs called *P W Years*. The reason I can't finish them is because I spend half the time watching you and De Klerk on TV. You guys really are wonderful on the box.

Mandela: Now that you've mentioned De Klerk, what do you think of the man? Do you think he's a man of integrity?

Botha: He's quite a nice guy, you know, but you guys are pretty rough on him. You've called him all sorts of things, from a murderer to a lame duck president. No wonder he thinks you are playing the man rather than the ball.

Mandela: This is very surprising, coming from a man who has had the guts to tell people that politics is not for sissies. Well, he ain't seen nothing yet. Wait until I unleash my cracking at the end of this election campaign. He'd wish he was never born. Enough of that, I wanted to ask you: Remember the Rubicon? Since you're the man who first saw it, do you think we have crossed it?

Botha: Read my lips. You've to turn and look behind you if you want to see the Rubicon.

Mandela: What possible advice can you give a man who has never seen the inside of parliamentary politics – a man like myself?

Botha: It's the ability to know when to retire. My time came and I refused to believe it had. I was so embarrassed when Pik and his friends forcibly removed me from office. When I think about it, I feel very miserable. So, watch out!

Mandela: Sorry, I didn't want you to dwell in the past. My time is running out and I now have to get going. It was nice talking to you.

Botha: Thank you for dropping by. I really appreciate it. Sorry, before you go, I wanted to tell you something.

Mandela: What is it?

Botha: I like the way you dress. You really have expensive taste. On that score, you're one up on poor F W.

Mandela: You know, I don't even think about it. Thank you, anyway.

1995's New Year resolutions

The beginning of the new year is a time when many people would normally look at themselves anew, rearrange their priorities and redirect their energies towards ventures and projects that would change their lives and those of others. Making New Year resolutions is not an easy task as many people know they will never fulfil them. Politicians and other high profile sporting and showbiz personalities deliberately avoid making New Year resolutions for fear of embarrassing themselves as the year progresses. But we, the people on the ground, want them to tell us what exactly they have in store for us in the New Year. Because we know they are damn scared of making commitments, we have decided to select a few people who make our world go round, put words into their mouths and commit them to at least doing something constructive and worthwhile.

Minister of Health, Dr Nkosazana Zuma: 'As Minister of Health, my top priority is to persuade comrade Deputy President Thabo Mbeki to quit smoking. It is not only a bad habit – it kills. If comrade Thabo persists, I swear not to attend his funeral if he dies of lung cancer.'

Deputy President Thabo Mbeki: 'The so-called Thabo Mbeki Escapades are now a thing of the past. I swear I'll never go missing again in Africa or anywhere else. As for smoking my pipe, forget it, because every time I smoke it, I feel like I'm smoking a peace pipe. Peace is something we are still in dire need of in the new South Africa.'

Soccer coach Stanley 'Screamer' Tshabalala: 'I've withdrawn my application for a boxing licence and will concentrate

on what I know best – coaching, and not journalist bash-
ing. So, all is forgiven, Sy Lerman.'

TV chat show host Dali Tambo: 'One of my most ambitious
plans this year is to invite Minister of Home Affairs
Chief Mangosuthu Buthelezi to the *People of the South*
studio before he thinks of storming it. I'll try and make

him as comfortable as possible by talking to him in Zulu which, believe it or not, I speak with proficiency and authority since coming back home from London.'

Sipho 'Hotstix' Mabuse: 'I resolve to stop playing my old and tired songs, such as *Jive Soweto*, in live concerts and TV shows, and release a new chart-busting album instead.'

Eastern Cape Premier Raymond Mhlaba: 'I will quit my position as premier of the Eastern Cape. I under-estimated the demands of the job when I accepted the position. It's one thing to be a veteran of the struggle and another to be a good administrator.'

Miss South Africa, Basetsane Makgalemele: 'I'll buy a CD with the song entitled *Forever Young*.'

SABC Chief Executive Zwelakhe Sisulu: 'I must confess that I still prefer the written word to the spoken word. I'm not making any bold predictions but I may go back to newspapers before the year is out.'

King Goodwill Zwelithini: 'I will finally formally join the African National Congress. This business of not being politically non-aligned just does not work.'

My long-suffering husband

As part of its International Women's Day celebrations, the African National Congress once published a full-page advert highlighting the suffering faced by women every hour of their waking lives. But as woman power sweeps across the globe, threatening to blow man into extinction, no one is paying particular attention to the hardship and pain experienced by men on this troubled earth. (The Lorena Bobbitt saga is a case in point.) Seeing that the United Nations is, deliberately or otherwise, turning a blind eye to man's suffering, I and my friends declare March 16 the International Day of Man. The aim is to prevent man, who is already being outnumbered in South Africa, from becoming an endangered species. For the sake of balance, we publish what we deem to be the male version of the ANC advert:

6.00 pm: He arrives home from work, extremely exhausted. This being pay day, wifey empties his pockets until she has squeezed the last cent out of him.

7.00 pm: Wifey reminds him it is his turn to cook even though he did so the previous day, the day before, and the day before the day before. He misses the news on TV.

8.00 pm: He prepares the table but is then told to leave everything and change the baby's nappy. He loses his appetite.

9.00 pm: He tries to read his newspaper. Mother-in-law is dropped at the gate by a 'special delivery' taxi as it always happens on pay day.

10.00 pm: He goes to bed.

11.00 pm: He is woken up and reminded that it is his job to lock the gate every night. He goes out to lock the gate.

Midnight: He goes to bed.

1.00 am: He is woken up and told to go out and investigate 'a shooting' outside and a possible break-in. He finds it is a cat which had fallen from the tree.

2.00 am: He goes to bed.

3.00 am: 'Court case' starts. Wifey accuses him of having an extra-marital affair as a woman called Nomsa had phoned earlier in the day but dropped the phone after claiming she had inadvertently dialled a wrong number. Can he please clarify?

5.00 am: 'Court case' ends inconclusively.

6.00 am: This being a Saturday morning, he wakes up and prepares breakfast for the whole family.

7.00 am: Mother-in-law wakes up. He prepares breakfast for mother-in-law. He makes mother-in-law's bed.

8.00 am: Brother-in-law arrives as he always does a day after pay day. Brother-in-law doesn't speak to him but borrows R500 from his sister.

9.00 am: Man drops wifey, mother-in-law and brother-in-law at the shopping mall and proceeds to a parents' meeting at his children's school.

Midday: He picks up mother-in-law and wifey at shopping mall.

1.00 pm: Helps carry mother-in-law's groceries to her home.

2.00 pm: Arrives home to relax. Wifey tells him to fix a blocked drain and leaking geyser.

3.00 pm: Sister-in-law and her husband arrive. He is sent to buy a few beers at Lizzie's Inn for the visitors.

4.00 pm: Father-in-law phones and says his wife has suddenly caught ill and must be taken to hospital.

5.00 pm: Man drives to the in-laws. He takes mother-in-law to hospital. Father-in-law says he will spend the rest of the weekend with his son-in-law's family.

6.00 pm: He arrives home with father-in-law. Takes sister-in-law and her husband home.

Still in doubt of who is the president of the United States?

Why Americans are always wrong

Before she left South Africa, American journalist Kim O'Donnel told us in a newspaper article how perplexed and frustrated she was about 'this place called South Africa'. The gist of her article was on why South Africans didn't do things the American way. It is true that South Africa and the United States are worlds apart in terms of development but it does not automatically follow that the American way is the best way of doing things. After a two-week visit to the United States, I found the American way of doing things a little bit peculiar, funny and strange. I came back home with more questions than answers.

Why, for instance, are public toilets in the United States called bathrooms when in the rest of the world people simply call them toilets, public conveniences, or even closets?

Why is that clothing shop in the Gillard Mall in Columbia, Missouri, called The Closet?

Why do Americans, given the fact that they have a big drug problem on their hands, call a pharmacy a drug store instead of a chemist?

Why is takeaway food you buy at McDonald's called 'carry out', 'take out' or 'to go'? Why is tomato sauce called ketchup? Still talking about food, why do Americans invite you to dinner and still expect you to pay your side of the bill? Why do they call a bill a check and why is cheque spelt check? Why do most Americans always go for a second helping at their Sunday brunches? Why do many American newspaper editors regard the food section as one of the most important features in their publications?

Why is jewellery spelt jewelry?

Why are chips called French fries and why are chips not served with Russians? Why is a sub-editor called a copy editor or, worse still, an editor? Why is a sub-title called a closed caption? Why do Americans emphasise the last 'S' in the name St Louis when they don't do the same when they pronounce the word Illinois? Why is the last 'T' in Detroit emphasised?

Why is autumn called fall and why is theatre spelt theater? Why do they, when you order a Coke at a restaurant, fill three quarters of your glass with ice? Why were the Americans looking forward to hosting the 1994 Soccer World Cup when they knew they ain't a soccer loving nation and did not have the slightest chance of even making it to the semi-finals? Why is American football different from football as we know it? Why are auto teller machines called cash stations? Why is a discount called a break and why do they call a lay-bye a layaway?

My name is Tokyo, your host tonight

Gauteng premier Tokyo Sexwale made history when he became the first South African politician to host a talk show on Radio 702. The following is Sexwale's very first live show that you never heard . . .

'Good evening to all you 702landers. This is *Talk At Nine* and my name is Tokyo Sexwale, your host and premier of 702land, otherwise known by its politically correct name of Gauteng, the most powerful and richest region in the country. I must confess that since getting myself on the payroll of 702, I prefer calling the region 702land to the official name of Gauteng. You may have already noticed 702 billboards all over the region which say Gauteng is the Sotho name for 702land. It makes sense for us at 702 to call this region 702land. It's a unique name, the first of its kind in the world. People who live in 702land are naturally called 702landers. Now, what would you call people who live in this region if we were to continue calling it Gauteng? Gauties, Gautengese or Gautengers? It does not make sense, does it? Enough of that, let's get down to business at hand.

'Tonight's show, ladies and gentlemen, is an open line. Phone in and tell us what's bugging you. What's on your mind? Is it the water restrictions? Is it the drought or is it your premier? Is it the IFP or is it the communists? Is it the crime wave or is it the ANC, the National Party, the DP or the PAC? Remember, this station is in touch, in tune and independent. The lines are wide open. Just go for them. Oh! Before we go to the lines, my producer has whispered something in my ear. He says I must read out this commercial to you, dear listeners.

'The commercial, ladies and gentlemen, reads: "Come to the Free State, the friendliest province in the country, where people work hand in hand in a spirit of goodwill. Investing in the Free State is investing in the future." End of commercial and on with the show.'

Long pause

'Ladies and gentlemen, if I were to respond to this commercial, I would say the statement that the Free State is the friendliest province is not entirely true.

'Hold on, here's another commercial. It reads thus: "North West, the platinum province of South Africa, is the place to be, the gateway to Africa. If you are tired of the hullabaloo and the hustle and bustle of Gauteng, escape to the North West. You will be happy you did." End of commercial.'

Another long pause.

'My dear listeners, I'm beginning to hate these commercials and the unsubstantiated claims made by my counterparts in the Free State and North West. But I won't respond.

'Now let's go to the lines. There's a caller on Line 1. Good evening Michelle in Sandton, what's on your mind tonight?'

'Mr Sexwale, I'm one of your greatest admirers. Two years ago I was one of the housewives in the northern suburbs who voted you the sexiest man on earth, on this very radio station.'

'That's a compliment but what's on your mind, Michelle?'

'How about us going out for a cup of coffee at a time and place convenient for you? I won't mind to pay the . . .'

Line goes dead.

'Michelle's out of order. I cut her off because this is a people's programme. Here's another caller on the line.

137

Good evening Claire in Blairgowrie. What can you tell me this evening?'

'I want to thank you for everything you are doing for our region. But most of all I'd like to say to you that I like your voice. It is the sexiest voice I've ever heard. You make my . . .'

Line goes dead.

'I appreciate what people are saying about me but I'm a happily married man and a politician. Now, I know this is a talk radio where music is not allowed but I can't resist the temptation to play this song while people decide if they want to contribute constructively to this show. The song is by my favourite group, Boom Shaka.

'The song is called *It's About Time*. Perhaps it's also about time I re-thought my association with 702.'

Here is the unbiased news

Good evening, comrades, here is the news behind the news, the truth and nothing else but the truth as interpreted and passed by the editor-in-chief, Comrade Deputy President Thabo Mbeki and read by Khanyisile Dhlomo-Mkhize:

The South African Communist Party, a long-time ally of the African National Congress, the dominant party in the Government of National Unity, has increased its membership to more than two million people in five years. This fact was revealed by SACP general secretary Comrade Charles Nqakula at a rally in Port Elizabeth earlier today. We, however, do not have the visuals taken at the rally as the tapes did not arrive in time for this bulletin.

In Cape Town, the honourable President of the new South Africa, Comrade Nelson Rolihlahla Mandela, today dismissed suggestions that he was becoming buddy-buddy with the people's enemy, the president of Inkatha Freedom Party, Chief Mangosuthu Buthelezi. This false impression was created when a foreign news crew photographed the two men allegedly shaking hands and smiling at each other after a meeting at Tuynhuis in Cape Town yesterday. The picture of Comrade President allegedly shaking hands with the people's enemy was published in major newspapers across the world

Comrade Mandela was today quoted as saying: 'That picture is lying. We never at any stage shook hands. We were in fact squaring up to each other. The camera apparently caught us when our hands were lowered. I think also that people must try to differentiate between a smile and a snarl. I was not smiling at the chief, I was in fact snarling at him.'

In Gauteng, premier of the province Comrade Tokyo Sexwale said that contrary to biased news reports in the mainstream media, the Reconstruction and Development Programme was very much on track in the region. Speaking at a secret dinner to honour Comrade Fidel Castro of Cuba in Johannesburg last night, Comrade Tokyo said the provincial government had in fact built more than one house in the region.

We may not have built 150 000 houses since the May 10, 1994 inauguration but we certainly have built more than one house. I don't have the exact figures at the moment but I can tell you that the RDP in this region is definitely on track.'

Sports: We have nothing to report on today as the sport story we were supposed to air has not yet been sanctioned by the honourable Minister of Sport and Recreation Comrade Steve Tshwete. We will fill you in as and when the Comrade Minister is available to give us the edited version of events.

To end the news behind the news, the main point again: SACP membership swells to more than two million people.

TEN

Words Are Like Bullets

Your tongue, no matter how sweet it can be, can let you down at the most inopportune moment, irrespective of whether you are a respected TV anchorman with excellent language skills, a powerful orator or highly educated politician. It can get entangled in your mouth when you need it most. It will disobey your brain by saying things you don't mean to. What follows is a collection of boobs, if you would like to call them that, uttered by some of South Africa's well-known personalities when their tongues unexpectedly took a slip.

Slips of the tongue:

'The Tembisa Long Taxi Association ...' Jane Warden (now Hicks), TV1 news reader (Dec 1992).

'More than 7 500 jobs have been faced out.' On a CCV-TV news programme (Nov 1992).

'There is many, many policemen who has been found guilty over many, many years.' Captain Eugene Opperman, former Witwatersrand police liaison officer, on Radio Metro's *Person-to-Person Show* (Nov 1992).

142

'I raised the meeting at the Patriotic Front conference here in Lebowakgomo.' Nelson Ramodike, former Chief Minister of the now defunct Lebowa homeland on TV1's *Agenda* programme (Nov 1992).

'Fifa regulations state clearly that the colour of the cycling pants must be equal to the colour of the shorts worn by the player.' Mr Zacharia Mosehle, president of the South African Football Referees' Association.

'We have been in cages. We have been in trains and we have been downstairs.' Dorianne Berry on *Good Morning South Africa* after a visit to Stilfontein Gold Mine (Oct 1992).

'It's nine o'clock. This is the news update, good night ... nxa!!! ... good evening.' Desiree Makote, former CCV-TV news reader (Oct 1992).

'I've been seeing him monthly for the past month.' Former State President F W de Klerk on TV1's *Agenda* programme.

'At quarter past night, quarter past nine.' Rodney Trudgeon on Radio South Africa (Sept 1992).

'We have seen many wastes from Iwisa Kaizer Chiefs.' TV sports commentator Dumile Mateza during a live broadcast of the BobSave Superbowl knockout game between Iwisa Kaizer Chiefs and Sporting FC at Rand Stadium (Sept 1992).

'Thousands of Zion Christian Church members are expected to attend the September conference in Moira.' Isaac Phaahla, Radio Metro news reader (Sept 1992).

'I've been summoned here by attorney Mthethwa to carry out examinations on the patient ... eh? ... at least, on the cadaver.' The late Dr Jonathan Gluckman, top South African pathologist in a TV interview (Aug 1992).

'I've just received news from Harare, Zimbabwe, and those news are not good news.' TV sports commentator Dumile Mateza after the SA national soccer team was given a 4–0 thrashing by Zimbabwe (Aug 1992).

144

'We'd also like to thank the sponsor, Castle Breweries ...' Neil Tovey, first captain of the SA soccer squad in a TV interview before the team's departure to Harare (Aug 1992).

'Phillip van Niekerk of the *Weekly Daily Mail* was shot in the arm.' Frank Sesno, news reader, CNN International (Aug 1992).

'All our athletes is going to Barcelona ...' a presenter on a promotional programme on the Olympic Games (Aug 1992).

'You mellow with the wine.' Hlapane Masitenyane, CCV-TV commentator, referring to ageing Nick Sishweni during a live broadcast of a game between Kaizer Chiefs and Orlando Pirates (Jul 1992).

'This was after President Daniel Arap Moi bowed to domestic and international presser ... (pause) ... pressure ...' Rodney Trudgeon, news reader, Radio South Africa, on the first multi-party elections in Kenya (Jul 1992).

'In Sebokeng a man was shot by the necklace method.' Michael Findlay, news reader, Radio South Africa (Jul 1992).

'Choose your choice.' Actress Nomsa Nene on CCV-TV's *Turn the Wheel* game show (Jul 1992).

145

'The fact that we are upper from the sea ...' CCV-TV's Bongi Sishi trying to explain altitude to Japanese lightweight boxer Orzubek Nazarov (Nov 1993).

'... help in burying our bereaved comrades ...' Shepherd Mdladlana, former president of the SA Democratic Teachers' Union in a TV interview (Sep 1993).

'Both boxers is hard punchers.' Leslie Whiteboy in a TV interview before the IBF bantamweight title fight between Derrick Whiteboy and Orlando Canizales in Houston, United States (Jun 1993).

'There will be an ANC somebody there at the rally.' Themba Khoza, Inkatha Youth Brigade leader in a TV interview (Mar 1993).

'GMSA come backs to you, comes back to you rather, tomorrow at six.' Alyce Chavunduka, *Good Morning South Africa* news reader (May 1994).

'Was the route to the library condoned?' Reggie Morobe, in an interview with Witwatersrand police spokesman Colonel Dave Bruce on CCV-TV's *Newsline* programme (Mar 1994).

'The king is answerable to its people.' Themba Khoza, Inkatha Youth Brigade leader (Feb 1994).

'We cannot allow rightwingers to disrupt or even disrail the election process.' Former State President F W de Klerk in a TV interview during his election trail (Feb 1994).

'Five people were killed in political violence in KwaZulu-Natal. One of them died after a lovers' row.' Radio 702 news bulletin.

'I feel very nice.' A former Robben Island prisoner in a TV interview during a visit to the island by scores of former Robben Island prisoners (Feb 1995).

'That allegedness has not reached the administration yet.' Velaphi Ndlovu, Inkatha Freedom Party MP, on

CCV-TV's *Newsline* programme during a debate on the aborted KwaZulu-Natal police passing out parade (Feb 1995).

'You are not happy to see your son going out with a black man.' Potata (Faith Kekana) in CCV-TV's drama series *In the Name of Love* (Mar 1995).

'Because they left early, we were not able to held them hostage.' A Vista student in a TV interview (Mar 1995).

'We are still recognising him.' A Winnie Mandela squatter camp resident on the dismissal of Mrs Winnie Mandela as Deputy Minister of Arts, Culture, Science and Technology from the Government of National Unity (Mar 1995).

'The incident took place while a television clue was filming an interview.' Jazzar Raad, CCV-TV newsreader (Apr 1995).

'In order to be able to pay back the credit purchased from the banks ...' Billy Corbett, Director-General of Housing (May 1995).

'You are a schoolteacher at school.' Nomsa Nene in a game show on CCV-TV (Oct 1995).

'Our province is the most illiterate.' Aaron Motsoaledi, MEC for education in the Northern Province in a TV interview (Oct 1995).

Quotable quotes

Sex is like bridge. If you don't have a good partner, you better have a good hand.
Bumper sticker.

Now is the time for the disabled to stand up for their rights.
An ANC representative on Felicia Mabuza-Suttle's TV programme *Top Level*.

Make love, not babies.
Inscription on a T-shirt seen on a girl in Malamulele in the Northern Province.

Heaven won't take me and Hell is afraid I'd take over.
Bumper sticker seen on a car in Soweto.

I'm so broke I can't even pay attention.
Bumper sticker on a car in Lenasia, south of Johannesburg.

Don't be a nut, screwing is fun.
A sticker at a Fordsburg, Johannesburg, service station.

Don't drive too close as this taxi stops anywhere, anytime.
Bumper sticker seen on many Soweto taxis.

Don't womanise, condomise.
Graffiti on a wall near Baragwanath Hospital's Nurses' Home.

Credit available to people over the age of 77 and accompanied by their grandparents.
Notice at a shop at Highgate Shopping Centre, Johannesburg.

To all virgins: thanks for nothing.
Bumper sticker on a Soweto taxi.

I'm not tired, I'm not lazy, I'm just Bushed.
US President Bill Clinton at the National Baptist Church Convention in Atlanta, Georgia, during America's 1992 presidential race.

If you drink like a fish, don't drive – swim home.
Bumper sticker seen on a car outside a Soweto shebeen.

Men are like old cars. They make promises but cannot perform.
Bumper sticker seen on a car in Soweto.

In case of fire, please pay promptly.
Notice at Uno's restaurant in Boston, Massachusetts, United States.